BENEATH A
BLOOD-RED SKY

MICHAEL LISTER

PULPWOOD PRESS

Paperback ISBN: 978-1-947606-66-1

Hardback ISBN: 978-1-947606-67-8

Ebook ISBN: 978-1-947606-68-5

Books by Michael Lister

(John Jordan Novels)
Power in the Blood
Blood of the Lamb
Flesh and Blood
(Special Introduction by Margaret Coel)
The Body and the Blood
Double Exposure
Blood Sacrifice
Rivers to Blood
Burnt Offerings
Innocent Blood
(Special Introduction by Michael Connelly)
Separation Anxiety
Blood Money
Blood Moon
Thunder Beach
Blood Cries
A Certain Retribution
Blood Oath
Blood Work
Cold Blood

Blood Betrayal
Blood Shot
Blood Ties
Blood Stone
Blood Trail
Bloodshed
Blue Blood
And the Sea Became Blood
The Blood-Dimmed Tide
Blood and Sand
A John Jordan Christmas
Blood Lure
Blood Pathogen

(Jimmy Riley Novels)
The Girl Who Said Goodbye
The Girl in the Grave
The Girl at the End of the Long Dark Night
The Girl Who Cried Blood Tears
The Girl Who Blew Up the World

(Merrick McKnight / Reggie Summers Novels)
Thunder Beach
A Certain Retribution
Blood Oath
Blood Shot

(Remington James Novels)
Double Exposure
(includes intro by Michael Connelly)
Separation Anxiety
Blood Shot

(Sam Michaels / Daniel Davis Novels)
Burnt Offerings
Blood Oath
Cold Blood
Blood Shot

For Donnie Arnold
Thank you for all the support, encouragement, stories, and friendship.

THE JOHN JORDAN SERIES ON AUDIOBOOK

The entire John Jordan series is being produced on high quality audiobook. Start listening to these thrilling productions today. For more information and samples go to www. MichaelLister.com

JOIN MY VIP READERS' GROUP

Join my VIP Readers' Group Today by going to http://www. michaellister.com/contact and receive free books, news and updates, and great mystery and crime recommendations.

AUDIOBOOK

POWER IN THE BLOOD, as well as many other John Jordan mystery thrillers, is available in audiobook format.

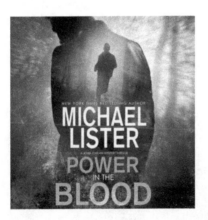

You can also listen to the entire unabridged audiobook edition of POWER IN THE BLOOD on Youtube by going to: https://youtu.be/1lcHaXcAmZc or the Michael Lister Books Youtube channel.

HUGE BOX SET SALE!

ALL of the thrilling John Jordan Mystery series Box Sets are ON SALE right now. Save big today only!

CLICK HERE to get the special limited-time deal.

AUTHOR'S NOTE

This novel was inspired by the real-life, true-crime case of Lauren Agee. My heart breaks for Lauren and her family and friends. Though Lauren's tragic death and the circumstances surrounding it moved and inspired me, this is a work of fiction, and these characters and this story are my own. Any resemblance to persons living or dead is purely coincidental.

BLOOD SACRIFICE

Beneath a Blood-Red Sky is a sequel to all the John Jordan novels that have preceded it, but none more than *Blood Sacrifice,* which I recommend reading first.

PROLOGUE

I n the early morning hours of Sunday, September 6, 2015, Blake Scott, Bri Allen, Kieran McClellan, and Brody Oakes left the Barge Bar after a long day and night of heavy drinking.

Canoeing back to the highest bluff overlooking the Apalachicola River, they climbed eighty-five feet to their campsite on the cliffside above.

Blake decided to attend the annual River Fest event with her sometime friend Bri Allen, only when plans with other friends fell through.

Bri had assured her she had secured them a spot on one of the many houseboats where most attendees of the event were staying.

However, when they arrived at River Fest on the evening of Friday, September 4, 2015, Blake learned that they were being joined by Bri's new boyfriend Brody and his friend Kieran, and they would be camping atop a dangerous cliff a quarter mile or so from where everyone else was staying.

To make matters worse, Blake discovered that the cliffside

campsite consisted of only one small tent and a few hammocks dangling precariously near the edge of the summit.

Following a full day of River Fest activities and a night of drinking and drama at the Barge Bar, Blake reluctantly returned to the campsite after being unable to find anyone who had room for her on their houseboat.

Official reports claim that the four campers climbed up to the top of the bluff at approximately 2:00 a.m. Depending on which witness you ask and when you ask him or her, the four young people either sat around and had a few more drinks or crashed immediately upon reaching their campsite.

What everyone does agree on is that at some time between nine and ten the following morning, Bri, Brody, and Kieran woke up to find Blake gone.

Though Blake is gone, her things are not. She has left behind her keys, phone, clothes, and the only shoes she had with her—a pair of Roxy brown flip-flops with black straps.

Though their statements and stories have varied widely, the three remaining campers claimed that they thought Blake had either crept out of camp in the middle of the night to meet her ex-boyfriend or gotten up early and gone down to participate in River Fest activities—even though they readily admit she never went anywhere without her phone and would need her shoes to traverse the terrain to get back down to the bottom.

In her various statements, Bri Allen claims to have searched for Blake and gotten increasingly worried about her throughout the day, but both witnesses and snapshots from that day tell a very different story.

Sometime after four that Sunday afternoon, Blake's body was found floating facedown in a slough—a small inlet river tributary that flows back into the swamp—across the river from the campsite by two fishermen, and following an incomplete, incompetent, and, some argue, criminally negligent investigation, Potter County Sheriff's Investigator Jasper Wallace concluded that Blake's death, while tragic, was accidental.

Dawson Lightner, an off-duty deputy providing security for River Fest and the first official on the scene, disagrees. And he's not alone. Blake's mother Kathryn Kennedy, a host of other law enforcement experts, and many attendees of River Fest, including Brody Oakes's ex-girlfriend Claire DeGarmo and Blake's best friend Alex Morrissey, are convinced that Blake was murdered and her killer got away with it.

1

"Thanks for agreeing to meet me," Kathryn says. "I wasn't sure you would."

We are seated across from each other on an old wooden picnic table on the grounds of what was once St. Ann's Abbey, the late-afternoon sun slowly sinking behind the tall pines on the western horizon.

"Really?" I ask.

The COVID-19 global pandemic continues to spread to every corner of the map, infections increasing at alarming rates —even here in rural North Florida—but since she has been in quarantine and I've been very careful, we've decided to go with distancing instead of masks, each of us sitting at opposite ends of the table.

"It's been so long . . . So much has happened."

She had called me earlier in the afternoon and I had driven here straight after work. No one knows I'm here, not even Anna.

I had started to call Anna to tell her, but didn't want to get into it with her on the phone—she has expressed more than a little jealousy and insecurity where Kathryn is concerned over the years. I realize now that I should have, and I'm feeling guilty about it.

I give her an incredulous look. "You really thought I'd refuse to see you?"

She shakes her head and shrugs. "No, I guess not, but . . . we haven't kept in touch and . . . the way we left things . . ."

She's nervous and uncomfortable and it's making our interaction far more awkward than it needs to be.

Interactions with former lovers are often inelegant, but this one needn't be as artless as it is.

Over her left shoulder and down the gently sloping hill is the cabin Kathryn lived in when this was a retreat center, the cabin where she and I had first made love.

Pushing her back into the cabin. Kicking the door closed behind me. Kissing her deeply. Spinning her around, pressing her against the rough surface of the rustic wooden door.

I had a brief but intense love affair with Kathryn Kennedy some twenty years ago, had studied and memorized the soft, supple curves of her body, the fine features of her sweet face, spent hours gazing into the brilliant brown eyes that were the windows to her creative soul, and yet if I had encountered her on the street now I'm not sure I would have recognized her.

Her kissing me back, asking in bursts of gasps . . . Anna get you going?

I had just come from the chapel following a fraught and frustrating visit from Anna, who had used delivering an inmate file as an excuse to come see me while I was on retreat.

Me asking, Is that okay?

Her whispering, Depends. She make you angry or aroused?

The cabin, like the rest of St. Ann's and Kathryn herself, now appears distressed and in disrepair.

Grief transforms a person like few things in this life can.

When I had first met Kathryn, her long, light blond hair had framed a roundish pale face with large almond eyes, thick arching eyebrows and plump pinkish lips between a tiny nose and a small chin, and a soft, curvaceous body. The woman sitting across from me now has been altered by far more than time. She is thinner and the blond hair framing her more angular face and sorrowful eyes is shorter and streaked with strands of white. Her lips, like her face and body aren't as full, and her porcelain skin shows the first signs of a spider's web of fine lines, particularly around her eyes and on her forehead.

Kissing more passionately, her intensity beginning to match mine. Hands searching, exploring.

Her asking, You with me right now or pretending I'm her?

You. I'm with you. I want you.

"I could understand you not wanting to see me," I say, "but I don't understand why you'd think I wouldn't be willing to see you."

My investigation into the death of Tammy Taylor had uncovered secrets and lies in Kathryn's life that created cracks and fissures in the foundation of her existence and caused her to call into question her very identity. And though it wasn't something I set out to do, the collateral damage caused by the case was not only painful for her but harmful to those she loved, and I honestly thought I'd never hear from her again.

"I get that," she says. "I guess what I mean is . . . I didn't expect you to be as warm and . . . I don't know . . . maybe . . . *open* . . . to me. I find former lovers to be more . . . guarded."

"I'm happy to see you," I say. "I'm sorry it's under these circumstances."

Fumbling with buttons and straps, zippers and snaps. Disrobing. Disembarking from the vessel that brought us to this place. Our clothes join in layered piles by the door.

As she is speaking, faint flashes of our previous life together filter through my subconscious to intrude into our current conversation. Like the lingering scent of an absent lover's perfume on the skin, I take in her earlier iteration.

Cold Cabin. Warm skin. Her small white belly sloping beneath her bare breasts.

Me saying, I feel like I'm cheating.

Her responding, Can only cheat on a married woman if you're the one who's married to her.

I had felt like I was cheating on Anna with Kathryn twenty years ago, long before we had gotten together, and I feel like I'm cheating on her now, not only because of the erotic memories rising unbidden from my unconscious, but from how attractive I still find this grieving woman across from me.

And I'm not unaware of the gravitational pull her grief adds to the dynamic for someone with a savior complex like me.

In our abbreviated phone conversation she had said she wanted to talk to me about her daughter's suspicious death—a subject I'm going to wait for her to bring up.

As if thinking of that earlier phone conversation has the power to trigger another call now, my phone begins to vibrate in my pocket. Without looking, I know it's Anna. I can feel her. Without removing it from my pocket, I reach down and end the call. A few moments later it vibrates again, notifying me the caller has left a voicemail.

"Well," Kathryn says, "I appreciate you coming. And I guess I shouldn't be surprised that you were willing to or that you're being so gracious about it. I'm . . . the thing is . . . I'm a mess and I know I'm not thinking straight. I'm desperate and I didn't know who else to turn to."

"What about Steve?" I ask.

When I left St. Ann's all those years ago, a relationship between Kathryn and Steve Taylor, the Bridgeport Chief of Police, seemed all but inevitable.

"I guess you haven't kept up with him any better than you have me," she says. "Not that I would've asked him anyway, but Steve's in hospice care. Final stages of pancreatic cancer."

"Oh no. I'm so sorry to hear that. I had no idea. Man, that's . . . I hate that."

She frowns and nods slowly. "He's . . . very bitter. Always has been with me, but now it's . . . everybody."

"I always thought you two would end up together," I say.

"He did too."

"Yeah, I'm pretty sure he's the one who gave me that idea," I say.

"He assumed when he did what he did for me . . . for our family . . . that I would be beholden to him."

Steve had ignored what our investigation had turned up and had manipulated the outcome of the case to protect Kathryn and those she cared about.

"And I guess I was. I gave it a try, but . . . We just didn't work. He thought we did. He thought we were perfect together, but . . . I was miserable. And we weren't even together that long."

Were they together long enough for him to be the father of her daughter? Based on Blake's age, Kathryn would've had to have gotten pregnant around the time I had been here or shortly after. I've been assuming that Steve is the father but it has certainly crossed my mind that I might be. The primary reason I haven't allowed myself to go too far down that particular rabbit hole is based on my belief that Kathryn wouldn't keep something like that from me—especially for this long—but what is that belief based on? Her novels? The brief time we shared?

"How long were you together?" I ask.

"The truth is we never really were," she says. "We went on a few dates. Hung out a little. He used to come here a lot. Was here all the time for a while. He acted like we were a couple, but unless he really didn't know what a couple was, he had to be just pretending, trying to will it into existence. I don't know . . . I think he really thought my sense of gratitude at what he had done, my . . . sense of duty or obligation or whatever it was would . . . win out over everything else. It didn't. And it only made me resent him. Anyway . . . we haven't spoken for a very long time."

"Is he Blake's father?" I ask.

"Can we . . . do you mind if we get into that a little later? I'd like to tell you about her and what happened to her and what has happened since then before we get to . . . Is it okay with you if I wait to get into that? Will you hear me out first?"

2

"Do you mind if we walk while we talk?" Kathryn asks. "I'm feeling so confined these days."

I tell her not only do I not mind, but I'd prefer to walk around the old St. Ann's campus, and we stand and begin to move in the direction of the lake, maintaining a safe distance from each other.

Safe from what? COVID or the gravitational pull of attraction?

The natural beauty of St. Ann's has been largely spared from the Category 5 hurricane that had decimated much of the rest of the region just two short years ago.

The small lake is rimmed with cypress trees, Spanish moss gently draped across their scraggy branches. Enormous spreading oaks and tall, thick-bodied pond pines grow in the bowl around the lake, on the abbey grounds, and for miles and miles in every direction.

Surrounding the small but ornate chapel at its center, St. Ann's consists of two dormitories, one on either side, and a handful of cabins down by the lake, a cafeteria, a gym, and a conference center with offices, all of which appear abandoned, disuse leading to disrepair and the faint signs of dilapidation.

When I was here before, St. Ann's Abbey had been a cross between a spiritual retreat center, a psychiatric treatment facility, and an artists' community. Prior to that, it had been a very exclusive theological seminary—and before that a Spanish mission.

Back then, St. Ann's had been operated by Sister Abigail, a wise and witty middle-aged nun who supervised the counseling center, and Father Thomas Scott, an earnest, devout middle-aged priest in charge of religious studies and spiritual growth. Kathryn, a young but acclaimed novelist, had been overseeing artistic studies and artists retreats.

"I raised her here," Kathryn is saying, "my Blake. She loved it here almost as much as I did. We stopped operating it after Sister Abigail died. Rented it out occasionally for conferences or corporate retreats, which generated enough income to maintain it. Since I lost Blake, I haven't done anything but try to find out what happened to her and who did it. It would break my heart to see the place like this if it wasn't already utterly and irrevocably broken."

I nod and hope my expression conveys my empathy and understanding. "I'm so, so sorry, Kathryn. I can't even imagine."

"I've often wondered if I'm paying the price for what happened to Tammy," she says. "If we all are. Look at what's happening to Steve, how much Tom and Abigail suffered before they died. It's hard not to think an overdue marker was called in."

She seems to be referring to far more than just Tammy's death, but I'm not going to ask her to elaborate.

In all my years of studying and observing, of working with both victims and criminals, the only thing I know for sure is that I don't know for sure how justice works. Sometimes I believe ultimately no one gets away with anything, that we reap what we sow—even if it's in the form of a tortured soul and tormented mind. Other times I think the nature of justice is random and capricious, that the innocent suffer as much as or more than the wicked, that the self-centered and sociopathic alike practice evil with impunity.

"I've never wanted to believe it," she says, "because I love this place so much, because it's such a part of who I am, but . . . maybe it really is haunted. Maybe an ancient, evil force really did enter and murder Tammy. Maybe that same force is picking us off one by one. And maybe I get to be last so I can suffer the most."

We reach the lake and pause to gaze upon it.

A gentle breeze ruffles the surface of the water and rustles the Spanish moss in the cypress trees. The deep pink streaks of the sun-kissed sky above are mirrored in the lake below, the two images connecting seamlessly in the vanishing horizon.

The scene before us is so exquisite, so heartbreaking and breathtakingly beautiful in the gloaming, that it's hard to imagine any amount of evil can exist in a world where such sights are even possible.

She turns to me. "What do you think? Is this place I love so much cursed?"

I shake my head. "No more than anywhere else," I say. "Every Eden has original sin. Every place is blessed and cursed, holy and haunted."

"Yeah, I guess so."

In many ways St. Ann's is a sacred place to me, my experiences here positive and profound, but I too had seen real evil here and am still haunted by certain encounters and experiences I had.

Kathryn and I had shared one of the most intense and transcendent spiritual and sexual experiences I had ever had beside this very lake, and yet on these same grounds I had come upon the crime scene of a particularly brutal murder, witnessed possession and exorcism and even a crucifixion.

I recall the afternoon Kathryn joined me here at the lake

with a blanket and picnic basket and entreated me to slip away with her into the woods. Through her passion and desire I felt the pull of the divine, echos of *The Song of Songs*.

Arise, my love, my beautiful one, and come away with me. See! The winter is past; the spring has come. Flowers appear on the earth; the season of singing has come. Arise, come, my love, my beautiful one, come with me.

As she led me away all those years ago I could feel myself waking up, opening up. I was seeing beyond what I could see, perceiving what was beyond the veil of what could be seen.

I experienced erotic euphoria as epiphany. As Kathryn and I made love, it was as if she had become an incarnation of the divine, as if God were loving me through her. It was a profound and mystical experience that included this place that would always be enchanted for me, and that haunted me as much as Tammy's death or any of the other horrific occurrences here.

Now as Kathryn begins walking around the lake, following the same path we had that day, she says, "Blake was the very best of us."

Did *us* refer to the St. Ann's family, to Kathryn and Blake's as yet unnamed father, or was I that unnamed father and it was referring to Kathryn and me?

"I know most parents probably think their kid is something special," she continues, "but Blake truly was. Everyone who met her remarked on it. She was just so genuinely kind and gentle. Had the most tender heart. And such a joy and passion for life. She…"

Trailing off, Kathryn begins to weep quietly.

"Kathryn, I'm so, so sorry."

Social distancing be damned, I step over to her, take her in my arms, and hold her as she weeps.

In another moment, she begins to sob.

I'm not sure how long I hold her, but after a long while she stops crying and I release her.

As I step back, she says, "I can't remember the last time I've been touched by another human being. Obviously, I needed that. Thank you."

"Of course. Wish I had been around to do it when this first happened."

"It doesn't get easier," she says. "People say it does. It doesn't."

I nod my understanding.

"You mind if we go back?" she asks. "I'm . . . just . . ."

"Of course not," I say. "Anything you want."

"I'm . . . suddenly spent. Thank you for understanding."

As we turn and begin to head back, I let her take the lead and set the pace.

"Sorry," she says. "I just got overwhelmed."

"You have nothing to apologize for."

"I know that finding out who killed her and why and even seeing them answer for it won't bring her back, won't begin to heal my brutalized heart, but it's all I want in the world. It's the only thing keeping me going. It's all I have."

I nod my understanding and try to convey my empathy though she is not looking at me.

She stops suddenly and turns to me, her sorrowful eyes locking onto mine.

"Please," she pleads, "please promise me you'll find out what happened to her and who did it."

"I promise you I won't stop until I do," I say.

"That's all I can ask," she says. "But it won't be easy. No one involved will talk. They all have lawyers and are hiding behind them. And the original investigation—if you can even call it that—is so flawed that you won't have even the most basic information you need."

"I'll do everything I can and I won't stop no matter—"

"And there's one more thing you need to know," she says.

"Your dad handled—well, *mishandled* the investigation. It was his department's case."

3

I call Anna as I drive away from St. Ann's.

By the time I do, I have missed three calls and received six texts from her.

"Is everything okay?" I ask.

"Where have you been?"

"I'll explain everything when I get home," I say. "Is everything okay?"

"I had a bad feeling and wanted to make sure you were all right."

"I'm fine. Sorry I'm running a little late. But everything's okay. I should've called sooner, but—"

"I was worried to begin with and then when you didn't answer or respond to my texts . . . You usually at least do that."

"I wanted to," I say. "It's just very difficult when someone I'm talking to is upset or if I'm in the middle of an interview. Everything has taken longer today than I expected it to. Are the kids okay?"

"Yeah, we're fine. I was just worried about you."

"I'm good," I say. "I'll be home soon, and we can have dinner and talk about everything. Okay?"

"You sure you're okay? You sound different."

"I'm just tired and a little drained from the day," I say. "Tell you what . . . I'll come straight home now and go to Dad's later —or even tomorrow."

"You don't have to do that."

"It's no problem. I'm not looking forward to talking to him anyway."

"Really? Why's that?"

"I'll tell you when I get there. See you in half an hour or so. Love you."

"Love you."

4

The jolting sound effects and haunting music sound particularly hokey coming through the small speakers of my phone.

I'm sure the images and footage on the screen of the YouTube video aren't much better, but I'm watching the road, not them.

For my drive home, I have pulled up the first video of Blake's case I can find.

Kathryn had given me a binder with copies of all the case documents she had in it, which I would dig into later, but she had become so upset and overwhelmed that she had been able to tell me very little, so I'm using my drive home to try to get a rudimentary introduction to the case.

As bad and over-the-top as the music and sound effects are, the deep, overly annunciated and overly dramatic voice-over is far, far worse.

"What really happened to twenty-one-year-old Blake Scott on that fateful night?" the middle-aged female voice-over actor is saying. "Was her shocking death just a tragic accident as law enforcement claims, or was she murdered as her grieving mother insists? On the final night of River Fest, she climbed this treacherous river bluff to this precarious cliffside campsite with three drunken friends to sleep in this small hammock hanging out over the Apalachicola River some eighty-five feet below. After more drinking and God only knows what else, the four friends fell asleep at approximately three in the morning. Six hours later, at around nine the following day, the others awoke to find that Blake had vanished in the night, never to be seen alive again, leaving behind her phone and flip-flops."

Kathryn says, "She should've never been up there. They lied to her and told her they were staying on a houseboat and then she got there and everything changed. These are not good people, and one or more of them killed my little girl."

The voice-over actress says, "The words of a grieving mother or the truth of what really happened? You be the judge. But Blake's mother, Kathryn, isn't the only one who believes foul play was involved. So does former Pine County Sheriff's Deputy Dawson Lightner, who was working security at the event."

"I'll go to my grave believing Blake went to hers as the result of foul play," Lightner says in a smooth Southern accent. "There's no other explanation. There's no way her body could've been found where it was if this was an accident."

I glance at the screen. Lightner is a thirty-something white man with a few extra pounds on an otherwise muscular build. His boyish face is intense and earnest and his short hairstyle is the kind you get in a barber shop not a salon.

"There were only three other people besides Blake up there that night," he says. "And one or more of them know what happened."

"Bri Allen, Brody Oakes, and Kieran McClellan were the only ones with Blake on the cliff that night," the voice-over actress says. "Is one of them responsible for her death? Did the others help cover it up?"

Pictures of the three early twenties kids are displayed on the screen and I take a quick look.

Brody Oakes is tall and thick with long blond hair and small, angry eyes. Kieran McClellan is skinny with dyed and sprayed skateboarder hair and his tongue sticking out. Bri Allen, whose tongue is also out, is a smallish bleached-blond with pale skin on a plain face, a nose ring, and an air of desperate neediness.

"Brody Oakes is a sociopath," Claire DeGarmo says. "Imagine the most entitled frat boy you've ever met and take away all morality and empathy—that's Brody Oakes. I don't know Kieran, but what does it say about him that he hangs out with Brody? And Bri is . . . Bri is the kind of girl who'll do anything her boyfriend tells her to."

The chyron on the screen beneath the attractive blond-haired, blue-eyed young woman reads "Claire DeGarmo is an ex-girlfriend of Brody Oakes."

"The thing to remember," Kathryn says, "Blake and Bri weren't close. The only time Bri ever came around was when she was between boyfriends—and that wasn't often. One of the abusive boys she was dating would get bored with abusing her and she'd come crying to Blake, but it wouldn't be long until another bad guy would come around and she'd go chasing after him and we wouldn't see her for months."

"I was shocked Blake went with Bri," Claire says. "They weren't friends really. And if she knew she was dating Brody . . . she couldn't stand him. He was always hittin' on her like everybody else. But she probably didn't know. No one else did."

"I can tell you exactly how it happened," Kathryn says. "There was a group of Blake's friends going from here and her friend Addie invited her to go with them—drive up together, stay in the same houseboat. At first Blake wasn't sure she could go, but then she worked it out. She bought her ticket but by the

time she let Addie know, there was no room for her in the car
or on the houseboat."

"I felt terrible," Addie Morrissey says. "And that was before .
. . what happened to her."

"Addison Morrissey," the chyron reads, "is a close friend of
Blake's."

I glance at the screen and see that Addie is an early twenties
African-American woman with huge black eyes, a sweet, round
face, and beaded braids that disappear into a bun.

"But we didn't have any room," she is saying. "Had two
extras on the houseboat as it was. 'Course, I'd'a known what
was gonna happen, I'd'a kicked somebody's ass off. Worst part
about it . . . Blake begged me at the bar that night to go back
with us. She really didn't want to be up there on that cliff with
them. She was hoping someone had gone home early so we'd
have room for her, but . . . we just didn't have room. I just . . . If I
could go back and redo it, I'd do anything to . . . I'd'a gladly
given her my spot."

"She should've never been with Bri, Brody, and Kieran,"
Kathryn says. "Should've never been up on that cliff. None of
this should've ever happened. And Bri wants to say what good
friends they were and how sorry she is that this happened . . .
Then ask her why she didn't look for my Blake, why she went to
the River Fest events that day and had a big time drinking and
skiing and partying while her *good* friend was missing."

The voice-over actress cuts in and says in her deepest, most
dramatic voice, "Blake Scott went missing sometime Saturday
night, but her body wasn't discovered until late Sunday afternoon. Bri Allen, Brody Oakes, and Kieran McClellan, seen here
in pictures posted from the final day of River Fest, spent the day
drinking and tubing and paddle boarding and jet skiing and
most of all partying, even as their friend who was with them
the night before has vanished. They later tell authorities they
thought she either hooked up with her old boyfriend, joined

another group of friends, or went home early, but Blake's keys, phone, flip-flops, and clothes were on the ground next to the tent where she left them the night before."

"Ask Bri why her boyfriend and Kieran did the same, why even after her body was discovered they continued to party and why Kieran posted that it was the *best weekend ever*. Ask her why none of them ever reached out to me, why they didn't come to her funeral, and why in the wrongful death suit they all pleaded the Fifth in their depositions."

"They claim they thought she may have gone off with her ex-boyfriend," Claire DeGarmo says, "but she had no interest in him whatsoever. They were still friends but that's it. He was there with his girlfriend. They didn't really think that—any more than they thought she left the campsite without telling them and left behind her phone and the only shoes she had with her. They knew exactly where she was because they put her there after they did what they did to her. And I'm not saying I know what happened, because I don't, but whatever it was, they were responsible. They're covering up something. I'm not saying it's murder. It could've been . . . There's so many things it could've been. Kieran could've tried something with her and got violent when she shut him down. She and Bri could've fought because Brody hit on her. One or both of the guys could've raped her or tried to and she could've fallen and hit her head while trying to get away. Or they could've straight-up raped her and murdered her. But whatever it was, they're all three covering it up."

Addie Morrissey says, "There's a picture of Blake and Kieran sitting in the hammock together."

The picture is shown on the screen.

"Everybody's making something of it," she continues, "because the three of them said she slept in that hammock with Kieran and he claims they had sex, but there's no way she did. Not consensually. She had a boyfriend. She was so happy with him. And she told me in the bar that night that Kieran got on her nerves. Creeped her out. Think about it. She's begging to go with me because she doesn't want to be with them or is even scared of them, and then she's gonna go back up there and have sex with him and sleep in that same little hammock with his pervy little ass? I don't think so. And he's a skinny white boy and all, but they couldn't both fit in that hammock. Hell, his hair could barely fit in it by itself."

"I'm not saying I know exactly what happened to her up there on that cliff," Kathryn says, "but I know who does. And so does everyone else. There were only four people up there that night. I don't know who killed her and I don't know who helped cover it up, but they do. And for all the people who say I'm just a grieving mother looking for someone to blame for what was a tragic accident, I say it's impossible to fall off that cliff and wind up in the water and it's impossible for a body to float to the place where it was discovered. And why wasn't there water in her lungs and why did her body float instead of sink? And why do people who claim to be Blake's friend and innocent of any wrongdoing plead the Fifth?"

5

"You didn't take my calls because you were with your ex-girlfriend?" Anna says.

Nash looks up from his homework, then quickly back down.

Nash Carter is a fourteen-year-old troubled teen who I had been mentoring when his mother was murdered—at which point Anna and I had adopted him. He has responded well to our love and being a part of our family, and seems less troubled today than when I first met him—though I know there is still plenty of hurt and anger lurking beneath the seemingly smooth surface of his being.

Anna and I are talking in the kitchen as I help her finish dinner. Nash is in the living room just a few feet away. Taylor is in her room playing. Johanna is at her mom's.

I'm buttering rolls on a cookie sheet as Anna places the final ingredients of her special no-recipe, no-measuring stir-fry into the large cast-iron skillet that had been a wedding present from an aunt of hers I had never met. The rich aroma of garlic, onions, and peppers fills this end of the house and heightens my appetite.

"Anna," I say, speaking softly in hopes she'll do the same, "you know that's not why. I wouldn't've answered when anyone was that upset and in the middle of talking to me about it. And just like always, I called you back as soon as I could."

"She must have been upset a long time," she says. "Took you a while to call me back."

"It only seemed long because you were worried."

"And now I know why."

"Really?"

"How else do you explain it?"

"I don't know, a global pandemic going on, my high-risk job, not being able to get me right away."

"No, I'm pretty sure it's the ex-girlfriend."

Her voice has the slightest hint of playfulness in it, which gives me a modicum of hope.

I raise my eyebrows and shoot her a *you know better* look. "And she was never my girlfriend."

"Which is worse," she says. "Y'all didn't get the chance for a relationship to unfold naturally, so there's the question of what might have been hanging over everything."

She's not wrong, but I would never tell her that.

"I know *what might have been*," I say. "Same thing that happened in every other relationship. It wouldn't have lasted because she's not you."

Her eyes widen slightly and shimmer with a hint of warmth.

"Well, what was she so upset about and why did she want to see you?"

I tell her.

"I'm not sure how I feel about you working a case for an old girlfriend," Anna says.

"Oh, I bet you know *exactly* how you feel about it," I say. "And I really wish you'd stop calling her my girlfriend."

"I know I'm being . . ." She trails off without ever saying exactly what she's admitting to being. "But think about it. This is coming on the backdrop of our breakup and my medical issues and . . ."

I start to ask her if she'd prefer for me not to take the case, but I'm afraid she'll say yes.

She shakes her head and twists her lips up and gives me a little shrug. "I guess I'm still feeling a little more insecure than I realized."

"I understand," I say. "And I get what you're saying about the timing."

"I just wish you would've told me before you went," she says.

"I should have," I say. "I'm sorry I didn't."

I don't have a good reason for why I didn't. Hoping she doesn't ask me why I didn't, I say, "You know you have absolutely nothing to worry about. I love you. I'm committed to *you,* to our family."

"What the hell, John?" she says. "*Committed* to me? Really?"

"I didn't mean it like that and you know it. I said I love you first. I'm just trying to reassure you."

"I want your fire, your passion, your—"

"You have it."

"I want your desire. Not your commitment. I want to be the only woman in the world."

"You are. That's what I'm saying. I'm sorry I used the C word. It's true, but it's not even close to the main reason you don't have anything to worry about. Anna, I've loved you my entire life. You have always been the only woman in the world as far as I'm—"

She tilts her head and raises her eyebrows. "Clearly that's not the case, or we wouldn't be having this conversation."

I shake my head. "Okay," I say, throwing my hands up in

surrender. "*Uncle.* I give up. I can't go back and undo being involved with someone while you were *married* to someone else."

I step into the living room. "How was your day, Nash?"

He shrugs. "Okay."

"Need any help with your homework?"

"Yeah, but none you can help me with," he says. "It's trig."

"I can help with that," I say. "I can call Zaire."

Zaire Monroe is my closest friend Merrill's wife and a medical doctor and math whiz.

He laughs. "Natalie may come over later so we can study together if that's okay."

I glance back at Anna, who gives me a raised eyebrow smile.

"Sure," I say. "She's welcome anytime."

"Cool," he says. "Thanks."

"Hey, did any of my and Anna's conversation bother you?"

He shakes his head.

"It was just a discussion," I say. "Nothing more. Everything is good. Just want to make sure you know that."

"I do."

"Whole thing could've been avoided if I had just called before I ever went—"

"To meet with your *ex-girlfriend*," he says with a smile.

LATER IN THE EVENING, after we had eaten and cleaned the kitchen, and while Anna is taking a bath and Nash and Natalie are doing homework at the kitchen table, Taylor and I are in her room playing, Johanna joining us via Skype on my iPad.

As we play and talk and interact, I am overwhelmed with love and gratitude for them—and grief for Blake and Kathryn. My ordinarily heightened sense of Taylor and Johanna's vulnerability is on overdrive and I pray for their protection with every breath, between every word.

In addition to everything else, and as kind of dissonant counterforce, I am filled with rage at Blake's as yet unidentified killer, possessed by a desire to bring him to justice, overcome with a burning ache to beat him to death with my bare fists.

6

"Tell me about the case," Anna says.

We are in bed. I am sitting up, propped on pillows, bedside lamp on, reading through the binder Kathryn had given me. Anna is lying next to me reading *Conscious* by Annaka Harris.

Taylor is fast asleep in her room across from ours, and Nash, the night owl, has been in his room upstairs a while, but is probably not asleep.

"Blake Scott," I say, looking up from the binder, "a twenty-one-year-old Florida State student went to River Fest with a foul weather friend, her friend's bad-boy boyfriend, and a friend of the boyfriend she had never met."

As I begin to talk, she tents the small black book between her breasts and gives me her full attention, looking up at me with brilliant brown eyes so deep I could dive into them.

"She was supposed to go with another group, but found out they didn't have room for her after she had already bought her ticket," I continue. "So she goes with Bri Allen, who tells her there's room on their houseboat for her, but when they get there, Blake discovers that they don't have a houseboat at all, and are instead camping at the top of a cliff. The makeshift camp consists of a single tent that only sleeps two and a few hammocks hanging from trees near the edge of the river ravine. It's obvious Blake doesn't want to stay there, and she even asks a few friends if she can stay with them, but no one has room. There are a lot of conflicting reports on what all happened during the event, which I'm just getting into now, but there was definitely some typical college-kid drama. There's a ton of drinking. There are fights. There are accidents and injuries. And any of these things could've factored into what happened to Blake. I just don't know enough about them yet."

"God, how can we let our girls out into this world?" she says.

"There was plenty of time for plenty to happen," I say. "They arrived on Friday evening and had all night Friday night, all day Saturday, all Saturday night. Blake, Bri, Brody, and Kieran left the Barge Bar at around two and went back to their camp. I'm not sure what all happened, but I think they drank some more. Some of them may have done some drugs. Not sure what else. At some point they claim they went to bed—Brody and Bri in the tent, Blake and Kieran out in the hammocks, maybe even the same hammock. But their statements are all over the place and they continue to contradict each other and themselves. According to the other three, they wake up the next morning to find Blake gone. Sometimes they claim they were worried about her. Others they say they figured she left to go hook up with her old boyfriend or join another friend group. At one point they said they even thought she may have left the event and driven home. The thing is . . . all her things were there—her flip-flops, which were the only shoes she had, her clothes, her phone, and her car keys, which one of them had hidden the day before because they had been drinking all day and Blake wanted to leave and they claim they didn't want her to drive drunk."

Anna shakes her head and frowns. "She really didn't want to be there with them in that camp, did she?"

"Bri, Brody, and Kieran participated in the River Fest events all day on Sunday," I say. "In some of their statements they claim they looked for Blake, but if they did they didn't spend much time doing that. They posted plenty of pictures of themselves partying, playing, drinking, dancing, skiing—all happy and smiling, gesturing at the camera with their tongues out. At around four on Sunday afternoon, a fisherman named Cotton Carver and his son Sam discovered Blake's body floating in a slough around the bend from the campsite. Carver notifies event security, an off-duty deputy named Dawson Lightner, who he then takes to the body. As Lightner, Carver, and his son were looking at the body from Carver's boat—before anyone else knew anything about a body being found—Brody and Kieran drive up to the entrance of the slough on a Sea-Doo and yell, 'Is that our missing friend?'"

"They so did it," Anna says.

"There is so much that is suspicious about this death. The body is floating. There are strange injuries and marks on her. Her clothes aren't put on exactly right and her mother says they aren't even her clothes. The slough is almost directly across from the campsite. If she accidentally fell off the cliff into the water that night, as the three who were with her claim, her body would've floated downstream, not across the stream of the wide river and into a slough on the other side. There's no water to speak of in her lungs. And yet, given all this, the investigator in charge of the scene didn't keep the three witnesses separated before taking their statements, didn't secure either crime scene —not where she was found or the campsite. Didn't order a rape kit. Didn't preserve evidence. Said from the beginning it was a tragic accident and officially concluded after a short, sloppy, nearly non-existent investigation that it was a tragic accident. Initially, Kathryn accepted the findings, but several of Blake's friends who were there reached out to her, as did Dawson Lightner, all expressing their belief that foul play was involved and Bri, Brody, and Kieran were covering up something."

"You say her name with . . . I don't know . . . such affection or something," Anna says. "*Kathryn.*"

"I really don't think I do," I say. "I hope I say it with empathy and sorrow, but . . ."

"I know," she says with a heavy sigh. "I know I'm being . . . Do you think you could call her something else—at least when you're talkin' to me? How about Kat? *Kat* sounds so much harsher and less elegant than *Kathryn.*"

7

Early the following morning, I find Dad sipping coffee on the front porch of his farmhouse, watching the horses in the far field beneath the sunrise.

I take a seat in the rocker a little over six feet from his, decline his offer of coffee, and tell him I'm investigating Blake's case.

Following his gaze, I look out across the dew-damp pasture in the foreground, at the dark brown quarter horse and the white and chestnut paint grazing next to each other in the fenced-in pasture beyond.

It's so picturesque and peaceful here, so sublime in its subdued, bucolic beauty that it's difficult to fathom all we're experiencing as a nation—the high levels of anxiety, fear, political paranoia, and general unease, the civil unrest and protests over police shootings of unarmed black people. Plus the rising daily death toll being exacted by the raging global pandemic taking place just beyond the pasture's borders.

"That case is closed," Dad is saying. "It was just a tragic accident."

"Her mother doesn't think so," I say.

He shoots me a look that conveys his surprise and disappointment at my gullibility. "'Course she doesn't."

"She's not the only one," I say.

"Always people willing to tell a grieving mother what she wants to hear."

"How well do you remember the case?" I ask.

"Never knew it too well, as I recall," he says. "Wasn't much to it, and I . . . I was out of town when it happened and . . . I was out of office by the time the mother started . . . making so much noise about it."

When Dad lost his bid for reelection, it was in the primary in August, so as the candidate who had defeated him went on to face another candidate in the general election in November, Dad was still in office. In fact, he continued to serve as sheriff for four months after having been voted out of office. It was during that time—when many say he had already stopped doing his job, when he was depressed and probably already sick, and when he was burning through all the vacation time he had accrued over decades in office—that Blake died.

River Fest is held each year on Labor Day weekend. Not only was his department short-staffed when Blake was killed, but he was out of town during the first week of the investigation.

"Would you mind reviewing the file and making me a copy of it and us talking again once we've both gone over it?"

"I'd rather not," he says.

"Really?" I ask, surprised by his answer. "Why not?"

"Waste of time," he says. "My plate is full right now. And it's looking like this election's gonna be a dogfight."

After losing re-election to one of his employees, Dad had retired, remarried, dealt with some health issues, and worked a few cold cases that had continued to haunt him. Then, before completing his first term, the man who had replaced him stepped down suddenly and Dad was appointed to take his place. Now he was running for re-election again, this time against an aggressive, musclebound correctional officer whose primary campaign promise is to violate the civil rights of certain citizens—a promise that seems to be garnering lots of support.

"If I thought there was something to it, I'd make time for it," he says. "The truth is there's not."

"I think there might be," I say.

"You need to trust me on this one. I'm telling you there's not."

"If you never knew it very well and don't recall much now," I say, "how can you be so sure?"

"I remember there were jurisdictional issues," he says. "County line is roughly in the middle of the river. She went into the water in Potter County but her body was found in Pine County. We had jurisdiction, but Pine began the investigation before they realized it was our case. I remember that those kids were tempting fate by camping up on that cliff. They should've never been up there. They had been drinking. It was a sad but completely avoidable accident. So I remember enough. The mother feels guilty for letting her child be in that position, but instead of taking responsibility, she's looking for someone else to blame."

"I know her mother and—"

"Then you should counsel her to accept some responsibility and let go, not give her false hope of finding a bogeyman."

It has been a while since Dad and I have been on opposing sides of a case or even a major issue, going back to before he got sick and was diagnosed with cancer, and I had forgotten how awkward and uneasy it makes me feel. It's a stark contrast to the peaceful pastoral tableau we find ourselves a part of.

"Well, if you won't talk to me about it, could I at least get the file?"

"I'd rather you not," he says. "And I'm asking you as a personal favor to me not to investigate this case."

"I gave Blake's mother my word that I would look into it, and I've already started."

"That's a shame," he says. "It truly is. Hate to see you waste your time and talents like this. You're a good investigator—the best—but not even you can turn an accident into murder."

8

athryn and I meet Dawson Lightner at the Barge
Bar on the Apalachicola River.

The Apalachicola River, named for the people
who once lived along it, begins from headwaters in North
Georgia and flows to the John Gorrie Bridge in the town of
Apalachicola to feed the Apalachicola Bay. The serpentine
waterway is surrounded by dense and diverse river swamps,
sloughs, coves, wetlands, longleaf pine landscapes, flatwoods,
hardwood hammocks, floodplain forests, and bluffs. This wide,
wandering body of water, edged by cypress, willow, oak, pine,
and tupelo trees, is part of an enormous watershed that drains
an area of nearly 20,000 square miles into the Gulf of Mexico.
The massive basin is home to historically and ecologically
singular and significant forests comprised of the greatest
biological diversity east of the Mississippi, which even though
devastated by logging practices still holds some of the finest
remaining examples of old growth forests in the southern
United States.

The Barge Bar is a dry bulk cargo barge floating in the river.
On one end, four modified shipping containers have been cut

open and welded together to form the indoor portion of the bar. The other end holds a stage, and in between are tables and chairs and a tiki bar. This popular floating bar and concert venue is the center of most river events in the area, including fishing tournaments, holiday celebrations, private parties, political and environmental fundraisers, and, of course, River Fest.

An intricate network of metal grating forms a catwalk with boat slips on all four sides of the barge. Stairs and ladders lead up to the platform above. I pull up to it in Jake's boat, which I had borrowed to bring us here, secure it, and Kathryn and I climb out.

Dawson, who was working security here the night Blake had been killed, is waiting for us.

A little older and heavier than he was in the documentary about Blake I watched online, he's wearing jeans, boots, and a tucked-in polo shirt with the words *River Fest Security* on it. His boyish face lights up when he looks at Kathryn and his eyes linger on her to the point that she seems to become uncomfortable.

Kathryn introduces us and we spend a few moments talking about mutual friends in law enforcement and each other's cases we're familiar with.

Eventually, he leads us down the catwalk toward a nearby ladder.

Because of the COVID-19 pandemic and the closing of bars and canceling of events, the Barge Bar is not in use at the moment and is completely empty, apart from us. It's as if the global pandemic had become apocalyptic, and we're entering an abandoned ghost ship.

"During River Fest," he says, "every boat slip is full and each boat accounts for between four and eight people or more. The boats bring people over from the houseboats and some of them make several trips."

The Barge Bar is anchored in the center of the river, but the river is so wide here that there is still plenty of room on each side of it for passing boats and even other barges.

Because of bends just above and just below this mile-long section of the Apalachicola, and because it is so wide and surrounded on all sides by the thick, ancient trees of a river swamp forest, this part of the enormous green-tinted body of water snaking through North Florida toward the Gulf of Mexico resembles a large, secluded lake more than Florida's longest river.

Upriver from Pottersville, this part of the Apalachicola is in a deep ravine with high bluffs on each side. It's part of a state-owned nature preserve that includes self-guided trails through the unique and diverse terrain of longleaf pine and wiregrass uplands to the top of a steephead ravine. Callaway Bluff, where Blake camped with Bri, Brody, and Kieran, stands at over eighty-five feet above the river below and is one of the largest natural geological exposures in the state of Florida.

During River Fest, the Barge Bar serves as the boundary for one end and a big bend in the river for the other, with the houseboats lined up on the end closest to the barge. In between, which is a distance of nearly a mile, there are all manner of water activities—skiing, tubing, paddle boarding, jet skiing, games, races, cliff diving, sand mountain climbing, sunbathing, and, of course, tons and tons of drinking.

"The houseboats where most everybody stays tie up together about a mile upriver," Dawson is saying. "Nearly a hundred of them. Not all of the houseboats have smaller boats, so those that do transport people back and forth. We usually have between four and six hundred people attend. Some come for the event but don't stay overnight, but most stay. A few people stay in tents on the banks, but most everyone is on a houseboat."

We climb the ladder to the deck of the barge, Dawson being extra attentive to Kathryn as we do.

The ladder, like the barge itself, is old and rusty, but the bar itself, including the containers and the indoor area they form, the stage, and everything in between, is clean and fresh and colorful.

"So," Dawson says, "you'll be able to see everything a lot better from up here. Up that way is where all the activities take place and beyond it is where the houseboats tie up." He points upriver and we look in that direction. "And everything event related stops here. All the camps, the activities, the boats, the people, everything. And yet," he adds, turning to point to a high bluff with a steep cliff and rocky ravine about a quarter mile downriver, "Brody always camps at the top of that big bluff down there. It's dangerous. It's difficult to get to. It's outside of the event area. It's isolated from everything and everyone else."

"So he had camped there before?" I ask.

"Every year he attended River Fest," he says. "So about three years before the year Blake died. Every year he had a different girl, different friends, but he always stayed up there."

"You still work security for the event?" I ask.

He nods. "Been here since the beginning. Worked every year of it."

"Did Brody come back the next year after Blake died?"

He shakes his head. "Hasn't been back since. None of them have. Bri or Kieran either."

"And you said every year he came with different people?"

"A different girl every year," he says. "Except, get this, shortly after what happened to Blake, he married Bri and moved away. Last I heard they were in Biloxi."

"She can't testify against him as his wife," Kathryn says.

"Exactly," Dawson says. "Everyone who knew them said he wasn't into her, wouldn't be faithful to her, and didn't plan on staying with her, but then he suddenly marries her."

"From what I understand he's never been faithful to anyone," Kathryn says. "Blake told me he used to hit on her all the time. I really don't think she had any idea he would be there that weekend with them. I think she tried to stay away from him."

Dawson nods. "She did. During the day at the activities and here at the bar at night, she was rarely around any of them. Bri a little, but as soon as Brody came around, she was gone. She spent most of her last night sitting at the bar with Alex Morrissey."

"That's Addie's little brother," Kathryn says. "He's always had a crush on Blake. Addie is—was—one of Blake's closest friends. You'll meet them soon."

"They're good kids," Dawson says. "Just like Blake. There was nothing romantic or anything. I think Blake was sitting with Alex to stay away from Brody and the rest of them. And Alex was fine with it. He knew what was going on. Brody is racist as hell, so he steers clear of Addie and Alex."

"That and the fact that Alex could kick his ass," Kathryn says.

I nod, trying to take it all in and get a feel for everyone and their connections to each other.

"Anything stand out from that night?" I ask Dawson. "Any issues or altercations?"

"None that involved Blake," he says. "Like I said, she kept her distance from them and just sat at the bar most of the night. She got up and visited around some. Danced some. But sat most of the time."

"You said none involving Blake," I say. "Were there some involving the other three?"

"I just meant that we're talkin' about a bunch of liquored-up young people. Nothing but issues and altercations. But no more than usual. And nothing too out of hand. You know how these things go. Most of these young people are from the same area, went to the same school, so they have all kinds of history with each other. Everybody's ex is here—and usually with someone else, so ..."

"Blake's ex was here with his new girlfriend," Kathryn says.

"They were cordial," Dawson says. "Didn't have any issues. Blake spoke to both of them—her ex and his new girlfriend. They spoke for a moment and moved on." He turns to me. "You asked if anything stood out from that night. She did. Blake did. She was so beautiful—like her mother—and she ... she just kind of lit up the room. She was very outgoing and friendly and energetic."

He had looked at Kathryn when he said Blake was beautiful like her, his focus and attention lingering on her flirtatiously.

Back when all this happened, Dawson was probably only about seven or eight years older than Blake. Was he as into her as he appears to be her mother now? Does he remember so much because he had been paying such close attention to her? Had they been involved or did he hope they would be in the future? Is that why he inserted himself into the case?

"What else?" I ask, trying to return his attention to the night of Blake's death.

"Both Kieran and Brody asked Blake to dance and tried to buy her drinks," he says. "She politely declined them both. Brody got into it with several of his exes, especially the drunker he got. A few times it looked as if he was trying to make Bri jealous, but most of the time it just looked like he didn't care."

"How did Bri respond?" I ask.

"She acted oblivious most of the time," he says. "A few times it looked like she tried to flirt with some other guys, but Brody didn't seem to notice. But she did get into altercations with a couple of his exes—probably the ones she felt the most threatened by."

"I've always suspected something like that happened up on that cliff that night," Kathryn says. "Brody tried something with Blake and Bri went crazy."

"That's certainly possible," Dawson says. "Just ask Claire DeGarmo. Bri assaulted her. But . . . I can see Bri helping Brody cover up something he did. I'm not sure Brody would do the same for her."

"That's true," Kathryn says. "Brody's all about Brody. That's a good point."

"Unless they were both involved," I say, "and covering for her is also covering for himself."

"Think that's more likely," Dawson says. "But not sure why Kieran would cover for them. From what I understand, he and Brody weren't all that close and haven't stayed close since it happened."

"He's actually in prison," Kathryn says. "On his third DUI."

"Brody could've paid him off," Dawson says. "I understand he's done that sort of thing before."

"Did Blake, Bri, Brody, and Kieran leave together?"

He nods. "It was a little after two. Most everyone had already gone. Blake was waiting down there on the catwalk near the boat. Brody and Bri stumbled out to join her. For a while they couldn't find Kieran, but eventually found him asleep in a boat on the far end. They had all been drinking, but Blake didn't seem drunk at all. Brody and Bri were trashed. And Kieran was just gone. I think he was on something besides just booze."

"You think he was too out of it to have done anything to Blake?" I ask.

"Seemed like it," he says.

"But," Kathryn says, "if he really was, there's no way he could've climbed the cliff to the camp, and he bragged that he had sex with Blake that night—something I don't believe."

"I don't either," Dawson says. "Not consensually. It was obvious she didn't like him. He seemed to creep her out. She had nothing to do with him all weekend."

I think about all he has said.

A breeze blows through the ravine, rippling the surface of the river and rustling the branches of the trees along its banks.

"Do you want to see the campsite?" Dawson asks.

I nod.

"Y'all can ride over there with me," he says.

Kathryn shakes her head. "Y'all go ahead. I'll wait here. I'm not up for climbing up there today."

"I'll help you like I always do," Dawson says.

"It's not just the physical demands of the climb," she says. "I'm not up for it emotionally today."

"I can see it another time," I say.

"No," she says. "Absolutely not. It's why we're here. Y'all go. I'll sit inside the bar until y'all get back. Take your time. See what you need to. Don't hurry. I brought a book with me. I'll be perfectly content to sit here and read, and I really want you to see it."

9

"How long you known Kathryn?" Dawson asks as we ride over to the cliff.

We are in his boat. He is driving. Between the whine of the outboard motor and the rush of wind, it's difficult to hear and he has to yell his question.

"A long time," I say.

I don't yell and I'm not sure if he heard me, but I focus my attention on the looming face of the cliff.

It's even higher and has a steeper pitch than it appeared to just a short distance away.

The terrain of the rocky bluff reminds me of Stone Mountain in Georgia, and images of the Stone Cold Killer case flash through my mind. It's hard to fathom how young and inexperienced I was at the time. So much has happened since then, but time folds in the way of memories and it all seems like weeks instead of decades ago.

Dawson steers the boat to the base of the bluff and I gaze up. It's so high and so steep I can't see the top, and there's no way to get from the boat to it—not that it could be climbed even if we could.

Though the bluff resembles Stone Mountain, it is actually very different. Instead of solid stone, the bluff is comprised of sand, clay, and stone—more like the layered wall of a quarry than the single rock of a mountain.

"Just wanted you to see it from this perspective," he says. "Can't get to the top from here."

"Looks like you can't get anywhere from here," I say.

"Too true," he says. "Expert climbers with full gear would have a hard time with it. We have to enter from the side where the path leads up through the pass to the top. It's what they had to do that night."

He guides the boat over to the right side of the cliff face where the bank is slightly less steep and there are trees to tie up to.

An old grass rope dangles down to float in the water, and we have to hold on to it to pull ourselves out of the boat and onto the bank, our shoes slipping several times in the slick clay.

"Don't let go of this rope," Dawson says. "Not even for a second. It's the only way up or down without serious bodily injury."

He leads the way and we begin the slow, winding, treacherous trek to the top, having to pull ourselves up with the rope, at times leaning so far out we're nearly perpendicular to the ground.

The damp, slippery earth beneath our feet offers little traction as we make our way through thick underbrush, beneath vines, around trees, and over downed branches, debris and detritus.

"Hard to see how four drunken kids were able to climb this in the middle of the night," I say.

"Exactly," he says. "They had no business being up here. And wouldn't've been if not for that asshole Brody Oakes. Some theorize they never made it up that night or that Blake got killed on the way up and they panicked and tried to hide her body in the slough."

The climb is arduous, and it takes us nearly fifteen minutes to reach the summit.

"You can see why even if she had liked these people, Blake would be asking if any of her friends had room for her on their houseboats," he says. "But to go through all that just to get up here to be isolated with creeps..."

My heart hurts for Blake as I think of her trying to find another place to stay that night and being turned down again and again. She had been so vulnerable, so at the mercy of merciless people that weekend. It was unconscionable for her to be so unsheltered—to not even have a tent left her utterly exposed. The hard, barren ground of the cliff, which supports very little vegetation, is mostly sandy soil and scree above solid rock formation.

There are very few signs that humans have been up here—a few dirt-covered and sun-faded soda bottles and maybe the ashy-gray remnants of a campfire.

The top of the bluff is short and narrow—only about fifty feet wide and fifteen feet deep—framed by a dense river swamp forest on the back and sides and the cliff edge and the steep river ravine below in the front.

Two small sand pines grow about six feet apart near the edge, their root systems exposed by ongoing erosion. The storm water runoff that flows through the longleaf pine and wiregrass uplands waterfalls off the cliff down into the river below. Each tree has four small cords tied around it, their ends fat and frayed where they had been cut near the knot and left exposed to the elements. I picture the narrow quilted hammocks that have dangled here over the years, placed precariously close to the edge and tied to the two weakened pines by the cloth clothesline-type cord that is little more than string.

It's so much higher than it appears to be from below, and

though I'm not particularly scared of heights, I feel shaky and nervous.

It's breezy up here, the wind blowing down the bluff at a steady clip to the river below, and I have the sense that a strong gust could lift me and send me plummeting to a brutal death of blunt force trauma down below.

"You know that old saying, 'Red sky at night, sailor's delight. Red sky in morning, sailor's warning'?" Dawson asks.

I nod.

"You should've seen the sky on the day Blake died," he says. "The deepest, darkest red I've ever seen a sky—and it was that way in the morning and the evening. It was like . . . It looked like the sky was on fire and dripping blood."

From where I'm standing near the center of the pinnacle of the bluff, I can see that what I thought was the peak is actually a shelf that runs the length of the exposed rock face.

"You see it too, don't you?" Dawson says. "They theorize that Blake must have gotten up in the night to pee and accidentally fallen off the cliff."

"But if she did," I say, "her body would've been found on that outcropping, not in the water."

"Exactly," he says, nodding vigorously. "There's no way to fall from here and land in the water. The only way you might make it is to get a running jump, and even then it'd be iffy. You'd have to put some ass into it. But it begs the question, why would anyone try to jump into the river from up here?"

"Because they were being chased," I say. "Because what was happening up here was worse than the possibility of being injured or even dying from the jump."

"That's the way I see it," he says, "and I'm guessing the only reason the investigators from Pine and Potter didn't reach the same conclusion is that they had already made their minds up that it was an accident by the time they came up here—if they came up at all."

"Is there anything in the water right below here?" I ask.

He nods and frowns. "Yeah, even if you could get to the water from here, you'd more than likely hit something. There are more rock formations, some downed trees, and some other trash and debris."

I glance to the wooded areas to the right and left of the cliff.

He follows my gaze and says, "If she went into either side of the woods to use the bathroom, and it would make sense that she did, it's not possible to fall into the water. You can easily slip and you can even fall, but in a matter of a few feet you'd hit a tree and underbrush. Even if you fell and hit your head and were unconscious or dead, your body would get caught up in all the trees and underbrush. No way you'd roll to the bottom. It's just not possible. And I'm not just saying that because it's what I think. I spent several days up here with Kathryn's PI and a simulation dummy the same size and weight as Blake. We shoved it. We rolled it. We threw it. We tripped it. We slung it. We couldn't get it to make it down to the water no matter what we tried—not from the cliff or from any point in the woods on either side. It just doesn't work."

"Did you try it with a hammock?" I ask.

"You mean tied between those two trees where she was supposed to have slept with Kieran?"

"Yeah," I say. "I'm wondering if it's far enough out that she could fall from it, hit the edge of the shelf below and bounce out and land in the river."

He nods. "Not possible. We tried it several times. We even swung the hammock out sort of like a slingshot to see if with some momentum we could get some velocity going. Not even close. Always landed on that ledge and never even close to the edge of it—let alone over it."

I nod as I look around and think about it.

"I even climbed down to the ledge and dropped the dummy from there," he says. "Still can't make it into the water. There are other, smaller ridges, crooks, shelves, and outcroppings. I bet you we've dropped and thrown that hundred-and-ten-pound dummy off every conceivable part of this bluff over a hundred times, and not once did it ever make it to the water—let alone to the slough on the other side of the river. And speaking of, we put a floating dummy the size and weight of Blake in the water on this side—in several different spots on this side—and by the time it reached the other side it was a mile or more downriver. Sometimes a lot more. But never came close to floating straight across and into the slough. It's impossible. The current is too strong here. We're talkin' a discharge of about 16,600 cubic feet per second."

"The original investigators may not have investigated this case, but you sure have," I say.

"I think I've been pretty thorough," he says. "I've never been a detective or investigator. I was just a deputy, but . . . I didn't want to give Kathryn any false hope. If it was an accident, I wanted to prove it. I just wanted to get to the bottom of what happened. I've worked so hard and for so long on it . . . it surprised me she brought you in on it."

"She really didn't tell me why," I say. "Maybe I can offer something, maybe I can't. Sometimes a fresh set of eyes can help, but—"

"The main thing is finding out what happened to Blake and getting some justice for Kathryn if we can," he says. "I care about that more than anything else, but . . ."

"But what?"

"I really hope you're not planning on swoopin' in here and taking credit for all the work I've done on this case."

10

"Lightner has done a ton of work on the case," I say.

Kathryn nods. "He's been unbelievably invested."

We are back in my truck headed to Seven Springs, a small community in Pine County, to interview some of Blake's friends.

"He resents you bringing me in," I say.

"I tried to explain it to him, but . . . Was he . . . unhelpful?"

I shake my head. "He was very generous with what he knows and from what I can tell, his work on the case seems solid. Not sure you need me."

"He's not an investigator," she says. "He's done some great experiments with that dummy of his and the private investigator I hired, and he's kept the pressure on, kept the case going, but he's about reached the end of what he's capable of."

"He mentioned he's no longer a deputy," I say. "What does he do?"

"Event security, odd jobs. Not sure what all."

"Why did he quit the department?"

"He was forced out because of the stand he took on the investigation," she says. "He was a deputy in Pine County, but even when Potter took it over he was very vocal—critical of the job both Pine and Potter investigators did. He had no jurisdiction, wasn't a part of the investigation, but never stopped calling for the case to be investigated properly. And then after Potter ruled it an accident and closed the case, he kept pushing for it to be reopened. He let me know what he thought and eventually he discussed it with the media. Potter County sheriff calls the Pine County sheriff and he's disciplined and harassed until he quits. He gave up his career for Blake."

"Which was a very noble thing to do," I say. "He seems earnest and sincere, like a really good guy, but don't kid yourself . . . He's crushin' on you hard, and that almost certainly accounts for some of his motivation—even if the rest is altruistic."

"Well, none of us has a single motivation for most anything," she says, "and what we do is more important than why we do it—even if it's just by a little. Besides . . . I don't care why anyone does anything, as long as we get justice for Blake."

I nod.

"And just so you know . . ." she adds, "I am aware of it, and have been very careful not to lead him on or give him any false hope. And not just because he's a kid. I think everyone knows I only care about one thing and don't have time for anything else. And it's not just time. I have no desire for anything else. Since Blake was taken from me I haven't been able to write. I don't sleep. I don't eat. I have no sense of taste or smell. I can't listen to music or watch movies or television. And when I try to read, I go over the same passage several times, unable to comprehend what I've just read. And if all of these things are like that . . . you can imagine how shutdown my sexuality and spirituality are. He knows all this and continues to help."

"I'm so sorry," I say. "And not just for your unimaginable grief but for bringing up Dawson's intentions and motivations. I didn't want it to become an issue—but I shouldn't've said anything."

"Dawson was very fond of Blake," she says. "I know a big part of what he's doing is about her, not me. Maybe all of it. I don't know. And I don't care. What about you, John? Why are you helping me?"

"Because you asked me to," I say. "Because it's what I do. It's my calling."

"Is that it?"

I shake my head. "No, of course not. I actually examine my motivations regularly and am still not even aware of all of them."

She starts to say something, but not wanting to go down this path any further, I say, "And before you ask me anything else about my motivations, let's get back to the investigation. Who are we seeing next?"

"Two of Blake's friends," she says. "Her best friend, Addie, and a school friend, Claire. They've both been so supportive and helpful throughout all this and even outspoken—the exact opposite of her faux friend Bri. They were both at River Fest, for at least part of the time, and they both know most of the people involved pretty well. And before you ask . . . I don't know what their motivations are for helping, but I don't think either of them wants to sleep with me."

11

S even Springs is more of a community than a city, an unincorporated town with a handful of stores and families that have been here for a few generations. As we drive through town we notice that most people aren't wearing masks. Some see it as an unnecessary inconvenience, not understanding it's primarily to protect others—vulnerable people far more at risk than the masses. Still others have been convinced by those that influence them that the mask is a sign of oppression, control, and the eroding of their freedoms.

We meet Addie Morrissey and Claire DeGarmo in a small oak-tree-canopied park near a lake so Claire's four-year-old son, Corbin, can play while we talk—and so we can socially distance and not have to try to hear each other through masks.

The oak trees provide plenty of shade and the breeze blowing off the lake makes the hot early September day bearable.

Both young women are a good bit older than in the original news footage and the documentary that followed, and I wonder if every time Kathryn sees them she ages Blake in her mind or wonders what she would look like after she completed the transition into young adulthood. How would her career be going? Would she be married? Have a child?

"Look," Addie is saying, "listen . . . everybody loved Blake. And the only fools who didn't were jealous or threatened. She was this . . . ray of light. She was absolutely gorgeous—everybody could see that right off—but she was also just the sweetest, kindest, most joyful person you were likely to ever meet. And I ain't talkin' about that fake sweet shit so many white girls play at. She was real, you know? Like one-hundred percent."

Addison Morrissey is shortish, thickish, mid-twenties African-American woman with smooth skin the shade of heavily creamed coffee, huge black eyes, and large lips that somebody somewhere must really enjoy kissing.

Claire, who is pushing Corbin in one of four hanging swings, nods. "She really was."

Claire DeGarmo looks like what she is—a tired, young single mom who doesn't get enough sleep, rest, or alone time. Her blond hair is a darker shade than it was on the documentary, her blue eyes a bit more world-weary, and she's thinner— too thin, probably as a result of chasing her child instead of eating.

"Higher, Mommy, higher," Corbin says.

"I didn't know her nearly as well as Addie," Claire continues after pushing Corbin higher, "but being in school together you get to see who people really are. We were both on the volleyball team. I got to observe her in a lot of different situations. She was truly an angel."

"Thank you," Kathryn says. "I always thought so."

"She was also . . ." Addie says. "You know how some good people expect everyone else to be good, think everyone else is pretty much like them? She was like that. She was . . . She wasn't gullible exactly, but she was . . . I don't know . . . innocent."

"Faster, Mommy, faster," Corbin says.

"I don't mean innocent in some goody-goody way," Addie adds.

Addie glances at Kathryn. Kathryn turns to me and says, "I've told everyone not to hold back anything. They're not doing Blake or me any favors by sugar-coating anything for my sake."

Addie says, "She drank, partied. Was sexually active and wasn't always faithful in her relationships, but she was just a really good person."

This seems to be a more truthful and accurate description of Blake than was on the documentary about the case.

"A little . . . naive," Claire adds.

"Yeah," Addie says. "She put up with some shit from other people that I would not. I tried to keep an eye on her. Look out for her. Sort of protect her from her own goodness. Wish I would have that night. If I could go back . . . I'd give anything to be able to go back and . . . It's like I turned my back for one second, let my guard down for one moment . . . And it was the worst possible moment I could have."

"Did she ask if she could stay with your group that night?" I ask.

She nods.

"Higher and faster, Mommy," Corbin says.

"Okay, honey," she says, "but let Mommy talk to these people, okay?"

"I feel horrible," Addie says. "I'll never forgive myself, but . . . it wasn't my group. The houseboat we were on was already overcrowded and I was the guest of a guest—and the only black person—and just didn't feel like I could . . . The guy whose houseboat it was already told all of us not to even think about bringing anybody back that night. Said if we wanted to hook up with somebody, do it at their place. And the thing is . . . Blake's ex was already staying there with his new girlfriend, and they both still had feelings for each other. It would've been awkward, but . . . the whole weekend was awkward that way.

Everybody had an ex or two there. I just wish I'd'a been like, 'Fuck all that, fuck all y'all, Blake is staying with me tonight.'"

"We all wish we had done more," Claire says. "I know I do. I wish I would've made her leave with me when I did. Wish I would have insisted."

"That's so sweet of you both," Kathryn says, "but y'all aren't responsible for what happened to Blake and I don't want you blaming yourselves. I blame myself for letting her go with Bri, but we're not responsible for killing her. And we know who is."

"Damn sure do," Addie says.

"Who do y'all think it is?" I ask.

"I know y'all know more about the case and all the details than I do," Claire says, "but I know Brody better than anyone."

Kathryn says, "Claire had the misfortune to date Brody."

"I was young and stupid and so insecure at the time," she says. "But I know now he's a sociopath. He has no conscience. No empathy. He's the most selfish and self-centered person I've ever encountered. And he's violent. He hospitalized me twice. He's used to taking what he wants when he wants it and God help whoever gets in his way. I'm not going to stand here and accuse him of murder because I don't know what happened up on that cliff that night, but I'll tell you this . . . he's a very dangerous individual."

"I wanna slide, Mommy," Corbin says.

"Okay," she says, helping him out of the swing. "Y'all mind if we walk over to the slide?"

We all indicate we don't, and Corbin leads the way across the sandy playground area to the jungle gym.

"Yeah, I ain't sayin' I know which one of 'em did it," Addie says. "I just think any of the three of them could have, and it was probably all three 'cause all three're coverin' it up."

"Yeah," Claire says, "it's hard to get past that. I don't know Kieran at all, though he seems like a very troubled individual."

"His ass in prison right now," Addie says.

"But," Claire continues, "I do know that Bri is dangerous and violent too. She and Brody together are about as toxic as you can get."

With Corbin in a continual loop that includes climbing the ladder, sliding, then running back around to the ladder, we get a little more separation from him and each other and can talk a little more freely.

"Tell him what she did to you," Addie says.

"Brody is always flirting with other girls," she says. "Always. He'll do it right in front of his girlfriend. All during River Fest he was stumbling around drunk hitting on everyone. But some girls he targets and is merciless. He was that way with Blake. She didn't want anything to do with him and made it clear to him, but he never stopped propositioning her, harassing her."

Addie says, "He's the textbook definition of douche."

"During the week leading up to River Fest he was still messing around with me. We had to keep everything on the DL because if he knew, my dad would shoot him. And then, in typical Brody fashion, he shows up with Bri. I kept my distance from him, but Friday night in the bar he came over to me and started talking and flirting. Putting his hands on me. I walked away and he followed. I kept moving but he followed me all over the bar. I finally gave up and just decided to leave. I went out onto the deck to get some air and try to find someone with a boat to take me to the landing so I could get my car and go home. Bri followed me out there. When she came up to me, at first she said, 'I'm sorry about that. He's just drunk. Doesn't mean anything by it.' But then she said, 'He would never go back to you. Said you were the worst fuck of his life.' Then she grabbed my hair with one hand and yanked my head down and started hitting me in the back of the head with the other. Started cussin' me and kicking my shins. I was dazed, couldn't fight back. She hit me and kneed me in the stomach and started spitting on me. Actually spitting on me. I don't know if she was coked up or what, but it took several guys to get her off me. Even as they were pulling her off me, she said, 'You ever come near my man again I'll kill you.' I couldn't believe it. I was so . . . just in shock. I've never been so humiliated and embarrassed in my entire life. That's the kind of people they are. I wish I would've taken Blake with me, but I didn't even go back into the bar."

"She'll do something like that to her with everybody watchin'," Addie says, "what you think she'd do to Blake all alone up on that cliff if she thought Brody was tryin' to get with her?"

"I didn't know it at the time, but it turns out she did me the biggest favor ever," Claire says.

"Bet your skinny white ass she did," Addie says.

"Caused me to miscarry," Claire says. "Didn't even know I was pregnant at the time. If she hadn't done what she did . . . I mean I guess I could've lost it anyway, but . . . I would've been connected to that psychopath for the rest of my life."

"I'm so sorry you went through that," Kathryn says, "but I'm certainly glad you're free of him."

I nod and we are all quiet a moment.

Eventually, Claire says, "What if Bri actually caught Brody raping Blake and went crazy and killed her? He always had this thing about fuckin' me while I was asleep. Always wanting me to pretend to be asleep. He liked to choke me during sex too— went so far a few times I had to tap out. The times I tried not to I actually passed out. I don't know, I just keep thinking . . . maybe he raped Blake in her sleep, Bri caught him, killed Blake, and they're all covering it up— which is why they got married. I don't know."

"It's something like that," Addie says. "I guarantee it."

"He ever do anything like that when y'all were together?" I ask.

"Yeah," Claire says, nodding vigorously. "Bastard tried to fuck my sister with me in the next room."

"What about Kieran?" I say. "He claimed that he and Blake slept in the same hammock and that they had sex."

"I don't know," Addie says.

Claire says, "Blake had a boyfriend at the time."

Kathryn says, "Trevor King. He was a student at UF at the time and wasn't there that weekend."

"Thing is . . ." Addie says, "they'd all been drinking. We all had. All weekend. And we were all a bunch of horny college kids. Hell, we were up there to hook up. Should call that shit what it really is—Fuck Fest. I ain't sayin' she slept with him, but . . . the reason I don't think she did wasn't that she wouldn't— even with a boyfriend away at college. She just wasn't into Kieran. He annoyed her. I mean in a big way."

I look at Claire.

She shakes her head. "I have no idea about any of that. I didn't know Blake like that."

"Well, I did," Kathryn says. "And I agree with Addie. Blake was sexually active—emphasis on *active*. But I don't think she slept with Kieran. For one thing he was passed-out drunk before they ever left the Barge Bar. For another . . . everyone says how much she disliked him. There's that famous picture of them in the hammock. But they're sitting and it's daylight. I think Bri snapped that shortly after they got there on Friday afternoon. I think Blake's expression was for Bri, was about being at River Fest, not Kieran. Had nothing to do with him."

Claire says, "He could've sobered up just enough to try something with her in the middle of the night and she tried to fight him off and—"

"I'm not sure he was as drunk as everyone says he was," I say. "What if instead of passed-out drunk, he was just sleeping in the boat at the bar?"

Addie shakes her head. "We were there. Trust me. He was wasted."

Kathryn looks at me. "Why do you think he might not have been?"

"If he was, there's no way he could've climbed that bluff to the top of the cliff," I say. "Especially in the middle of the night. It's tough enough stone-cold sober in the middle of the day."

Kathryn nods. "That's true."

"Absolutely," Claire says. "It's so dangerous. When Brody and I were together the year before, I went up with him and stayed there the first night, but when we came down Saturday morning I brought my stuff with me and told him I wasn't ever going back up there—and we were in a tent, not hanging off the cliff in a little hammock. Luckily I was able to find a place to stay for the rest of that weekend. And it was actually Blake that helped me get it. That was when she was with Cameron."

Kathryn says to me, "Cameron Perry. One of Blake's ex-boyfriends."

"He was so nice," Claire says. "And so good to Blake. He actually slept on the porch of the houseboat the rest of that weekend and let me sleep with Blake on their air mattress inside. Got eaten up by mosquitoes, but never said a word about it. I only found out later from Blake."

"He's the one some people claim Blake was there to see," Kathryn says. "The one Bri is referring to when she said she thought Blake might have gone to hook up with her old boyfriend when they woke up and she wasn't there."

"Was she there to see him?" I ask Addie.

"She didn't go just to see him, but . . . yeah, she was looking forward to seeing him. Nothing wrong with Trevor, but he was down in Gainesville and they never saw each other. I mean, not never, but rarely. And as decent a guy as he was to her, he was no Cam. I think she realized how rare a truly good guy like Cam is. Cam was there with his girlfriend that weekend and

Blake didn't go to break them up or anything, but she did say she wanted to see him and . . . more importantly for him to see her. I think she thought they'd get back together eventually. She had broken up with him and he never got over her. I hate to say it, but Hailey, the girl he was with, was just a placeholder girl for Blake."

"I always thought that too," Claire says, "but they're married now. Have two kids."

"Yeah, but only because of what happened to Blake."

12

I drop by my office on my way to see Hailey Perry. I'm trying to catch her on her lunch break at the CVS and have a few extra minutes, and though I'm off this week, I like staying in touch with what's happening in the department.

"I'm glad you stopped by," Reggie says. "I was going to call you tonight, but I'd much rather do this in person. Will you push that door closed?"

Reggie Summers is the sheriff of Gulf County and my boss. She is a strong, tough, smart country girl with as many scars caused by horses as cars and men.

I close the door and turn around to face her, wondering what is bad enough it's better to hear in person.

"How's the case going?" she asks.

I shrug. "Just getting started, but I'm not sure there's gonna be enough evidence to build a case."

"Well, your friend is lucky to have you lookin' into it," she says. "And I'm glad to give you the time off to do it."

Is that what this is about? Me taking time off?

I've taken a good bit of time off to work freelance cases recently, but only because I had accrued the time to take. I work a lot of overtime, especially when in the middle of a homicide investigation, and until recently haven't taken much time off.

I have a good relationship with Reggie and feel valued by her as an investigator, and because of that and the trust we've built up over the past few years, she's given me an enormous amount of leeway to pretty much do what I want. Is that about to come to an end?

"But?" I say.

"Well," she says, "your ability to take so much time off and operate almost like an independent investigator is about to come to an end one way or another, and I wanted to make sure you were prepared—or at least making some preparations."

"I don't understand," I say. "Is there a problem? Has someone said something to you? I work hard and do a good job. I only take time off because I have so much of it saved up, and only when I'm not too busy here."

"I know that. This has nothing to do with me or us or your coworkers. If it were up to me, I wouldn't change a thing. No, this is about the election."

Like Dad, Reggie is running for re-election.

"There's no way I can win," she says.

I want to contradict her, but I can't. Reggie was appointed by the governor under some extraordinary circumstances. She is the first female sheriff Gulf County has ever had—one not elected by her constituents but put in place by political appointment—and her chances of winning are extremely slim.

"And I want to make sure you're prepared," she continues. "To either change the way you work if the new sheriff keeps you on or to find a new job if he doesn't."

"Haven't thought about it," I say.

"That's what I was worried about," she says, "and why I wanted to talk to you. If I can help you in any way, I'd be happy to—write you a letter, make some calls. I don't have a lot of connections or much juice, but depending on what you wanted to do . . . I might be able to help out some. What would you like to do?"

I shrug. "What I'm doing—and for you," I say.

"Well, since that last part's not an option," she says, "focus on the first. Don't be overt, vocal, or public in your support of me. And ingratiate yourself to him. Let him know he has your support and that you'd like to work for him when he wins."

I shake my head. "You know me better than that," I say.

"You need to," she says. "You have mouths to feed—more and more all the time the way y'all take in strays. I'm trying to decide if it'd be better for you if I recommended he keep you or not saying anything. He'd be a fool not to keep you on, but . . . I'm pretty sure that's exactly what he is. With your reputation and case clearance rate . . . he's gonna be intimidated and inclined to get rid of you. He seems like a petty and insecure man—so weak he has to constantly assert his dominance and flaunt his power."

"And you think I should break my own code for the chance to work for someone like that?"

ON THE SHORT drive from the sheriff's office to the CVS, I call Anna and tell her what Reggie has said.

"How sure are you she's going to lose the election?" she says.

"She doesn't even have a puncher's chance."

"Then she's right. You do need to make some plans and preparations. What would you like to do?"

"What I'm doing," I say. "Except I miss ministry."

"You minister all the time," she says.

"I mean more formally," I say. "I was most fulfilled when I was a full-time investigator at the sheriff's department and a part-time chaplain at the prison. Wish I could go back to that."

"Nothing lasts, does it?" she says. "Everything's always changing."

Driving down Reid, I see just how many businesses are boarded up because of the four feet of water Michael's storm surge unleashed on them, the buildings that are still in ruin and rubble, the shops and restaurants that the COVID-19 global pandemic finished off.

"Despite all our efforts," I say.

Suddenly, I'm overcome with sadness, a kind of melancholic nostalgia that seems to encompass all things, including me and Anna.

"I've got to go," I say.

"You okay?" she asks.

"Yeah."

"You're the best at what you do, John," she says. "You won't have any trouble finding a job, but Reggie's right . . . It may take a while to find the one that fits the best, so it wouldn't hurt to start putting out feelers now."

13

I find Hailey Perry at a picnic table behind the CVS in Port St. Joe with a paperback and sack lunch.

I introduce myself to her and, following a brief discussion on the joys and benefits of reading, tell her why I'm here and ask if she's willing to talk to me.

"Sure, I'll talk to you," she says. "And all it'll cost you is lunch. I'm sick to death of eating these cheap-ass bologna sandwiches."

"Where would you like to go?" I ask.

"Provisions," she says.

"Lead the way."

We cross First Street and step onto the sidewalk of the downtown shopping district.

As we walk down Reid Avenue toward Provisions, she says, "This is a real treat and I appreciate it."

"My pleasure."

"No one tells you, do they?" she says. "How hard it's going to be. You meet somebody and you think they make you so happy that you want to be with them all the time and spend the rest of your life with them, and then . . . two kids that you can't afford later, you're working a shitty minimum-wage job, tired all the time, broke as shit, carrying your bologna meat sandwich to work every day, just so you can barely see the person you wanted to spend your life with."

"I'm sorry," I say. "That is tough. But it does get better—or can."

"Not likely," she says. "Not without an education and no skills. Be twenty years or more before our kids are out of the house and on their own."

"What does Cameron do?" I ask.

"His job is a little better than mine, but not much. He makes more but has to work longer hours and is dog-ass dirty and tired as hell when he comes in."

"What's he do?"

"Works for a tree removal service. They did real well with the hurricane cleanup—well, the company did. The workers like Cam saw very little of that. He's losing his hearing from that damn chainsaw. His face, arms, and neck are always sunburned, and the work is truly dangerous. And he does it six days a week so we can struggle to survive. I know I'm gonna get a call one day that a tree has fallen on him or he fell asleep operating some of that heavy machinery and he's dead—or worse, crippled and can't work."

I nod and frown and try to think of something to say besides I'm sorry.

"Don't mean to unload on you like this," she says.

"No, it's fine," I say. "I'm just sorry life is so hard for you right now."

"My own damn fault for not going to school and for getting myself knocked up—twice. Never been able to say *no* to Cam. And it's costing me like a mofo. Can't believe how much I fought to get this."

"What do you mean?"

"Oh, you know . . . Work so hard to keep your boyfriend, to

make him happy, fight off other girls. It's draining, all the anxiety and paranoia and . . . you know, vigilance. And you win. You get what you want and . . . it's this. It's just ironic."

"Can I tell you something?" I say. "I know I don't know you. . . I know we just met, but . . . in the short time I've been around you—"

"You can tell I'm the biggest complainer on the planet?"

"I can tell you're very smart and—"

"I'm not smart. Obviously. I just read a lot—or used to—and have a decent vocabulary."

"You're very smart and insightful and reflective, and I don't think you're doomed to have a life you don't want to have. I really don't. It won't be easy, but it's not now. You can go to school or learn a trade or start your own business."

"Yeah, maybe I can get people to pay me to come bitch to them about my life."

"You got me to buy you lunch to do it," I say.

"That's just because you want to know if Cam or I had anything to do with what happened to Blake."

"Have you thought about what you'd like to do if you could?" I ask.

"Huh?"

"What kind of work you'd like to do," I say. "What you're interested in, passionate about. You've got to figure out what you want to do, what you want your life to look like before you can even begin to work toward making it happen."

"Yeah," she says, her voice heavy with sarcasm, "all I need is a vision board."

We reach Provisions, pull up our masks and enter the cool dimness.

Even through the mask I can smell the fresh food and the seasonings and spices that go into making it a fine meal, and the atmosphere is filled with quiet conversation and the sounds of actual glass and silver and porcelain chinking together.

We are seated in the only booth in the establishment. It is enclosed on three sides and has high Plexiglas, providing us additional protection.

"I got nothing against Blake," she says. "And I'm genuinely sad she died. And I think she was a pretty decent person in most regards. But she was there that weekend to steal my boyfriend. I'm not saying actually steal him that weekend, but she was definitely starting the process. And I get it. Cam's a great guy. And she realized she had taken him for granted and didn't appreciate what she'd had. She was real, real subtle about it. She didn't interact with us much, and when she did she was just coolly cordial. She acted like she was staying away from us, but no matter where we went, it wouldn't be long before she was in Cam's sightline—usually flirting with some poor boy she had no interest in. Even before that weekend, she had started making up little excuses to text him."

"How did Cam respond?"

"Like he wasn't interested," she says. "Like he knew as soon as she had him back she'd get bored with him and either cheat on him again or leave him again. But I could tell her hooks were already in him. He was already getting distracted and he started . . . He was paying me less attention, treating me . . . different. Not bad. Just not as good as he once had . . . And that's why I killed her. I had to. You understand."

"I'm not sure one lunch is worth a full confession," I say.

"Then I withdraw it," she says. "*Now*, if you were to take me to dinner a few times . . ."

"Do you think if she hadn't been killed, they would've gotten back together?"

She shrugs. "We'll never know now, will we? But I'll tell you this—even if they had . . . it wouldn't've been long before she'd've grown tired of him again and he'd've been back with me, and we'd still be right here where we are today in marital bliss and domestic ecstasy."

14

I find Cameron Perry in the side yard of a house in Honeyville. He's part of a four-man crew removing mammoth, diseased oak trees.

Two new-looking, huge blue Kenworth trucks with claws and black dump trailer beds so shiny they reflect like a dark mirror idle nearby, their fourteen massive tires having rutted up the yard and turned up the sod in their tracks.

As one man tops the tree with a chain saw from a bucket raised high into the sky from the white bucket truck below, another is using the claw to load the branches and sections of the base of the previous felled tree into the trailer of the truck it's attached to.

I've rushed here hoping to talk to Cameron before he has a chance to talk to Hailey.

After telling him who I am and what I'm doing, I ask if I can talk to him. I have to yell over or speak in between the revving motorcycle sound of the chainsaws, causing my communication to be stilted and awkward.

He seems hesitant until I tell him that I'm working for Kathryn.

He nods and leads me away from the noise of the trucks and chainsaws to a spot in the front yard not far from the road.

He's a shortish mid-twenties white man with small, squinty, intense blue eyes and disproportionately large forearms and biceps, presumably swollen from running a chainsaw all day every day.

"Feel so bad for her," he says. "She's a real nice lady. Always thought she'd be my mother-in-law. Got two kids of my own now. Can't imagine something happening to them."

I nod and tell him I feel the same way. "Finding out what happened to Blake and who's responsible won't heal Kathryn or give her closure—there's no such thing—but even if it helps a little it's worth doing."

He nods and we are quiet a moment watching the work crew.

"Owner of the property thought those survived Michael," he says, nodding toward the live oaks being removed.

Michael, the Cat 5 hurricane that ripped through here just under two years ago, didn't leave many trees upright. Millions of acres of North Florida slash pines were wiped out in a matter of a morning.

"Extension agent says we won't know for four or five years how many trees we really lost," he says. "Some are dead man standing because of the damage done to their root systems and other wounds we can't see."

"We all have those," I say.

He turns toward me, his small eyes locking onto mine, and then slowly begins to nod. "You have no idea."

I smile. "Oh, I have some," I say.

"You ever had somebody you were hung up on and couldn't get over?" he asks.

I nod.

"Blake's mom?" he asks.

"I think the world of Kathryn," I say, "but I was talking

about my wife. I'm one of the truly lucky ones who gets to go home to the love of my life every night."

His small eyes glisten, becoming little ice-blue ponds.

"I didn't get to do that," he says. "Blake's been dead all this time, and I still think about her every day. I'm sure I should see a shrink or something, but . . . it ain't like I want to stop."

I continue to nod, encouraging him to continue.

"I love Hailey," he says. "I do. But . . . it's different. I'm good to her and she's happy, but . . ."

Happy is not how I would have described Hailey.

"She's great. She's just not Blake. It's not right. It's not fair to her. But it is what it is. And it's obvious to everyone. It's not like I can hide it. I've been pretty honest with Hailey throughout our entire relationship. I mean way back in the beginning and pretty much all the way through—though I haven't said much to her lately. But back then she pretty much knew that if Blake ever wanted me back she could have me and there was nothing I could do about it. She said she didn't care. She said she wanted me the way I wanted Blake, and she asked me . . . she said to me, 'If Blake was hung up on some guy she couldn't have and was willing to be with you, would you be with her?' I didn't tell her—I just kind of nodded like I understood what she was saying, but my answer was *absolutely*."

"So," I say, "if Blake would've let you know she wanted you back during River Fest that weekend . . ."

"I would've gotten back together with her," he says. "No question. And the strange thing is . . . I thought maybe that might be what she wanted. The way she looked at me a few times, the way I kept seeing her everywhere. It was like she was trying to get me to notice her without seeming to try. Not that she had to do anything. I would've noticed her no matter what."

I nod. "So you think if she hadn't died you two would've gotten back together?"

"I really do, and that's what haunts me the most."

"Do you think she could've been killed to prevent that?"

He shakes his head. "No. I . . . I don't know why she was killed or even if she really was, but if she was it wasn't because she might have been willing to get back with me."

"You sure?"

"You mean Hailey?" he says. "No way. She didn't have anything to do with it. She couldn't have. We were together all the time. And we had all too much to drink. We crashed hard in the houseboat that night and didn't move until the next morning."

"Just because you didn't, doesn't mean no one else did," I say. "Just means you wouldn't know if they did."

"You think I'd be with Hailey if she killed Blake?" he says. "I've just told you Blake was the love of my life. If she killed Blake I'd kill her. If I knew for sure that Blake was killed and who did it, I'd . . ."

"You think it was an accident?"

He shrugs. "That's what the cops said, but . . . I don't know. Blake's mom and some others really think she was murdered, but . . . maybe she just needs to think that. I don't know. I *do* think those creeps she was with are—they could've done it. I just wish I knew for sure, but it's probably best that I don't. Hate for my kids to grow up without a dad."

"I understand."

The largest of the oaks' branches trimmed back, the crew is now sawing through the thick base to bring it down.

Circling the base of the tree, the two men use their huge chainsaws to make strategic cuts, slicing diamonds and triangles and wedges out of various spots to bring down the beast in the exact spot they want it to fall.

As they make their matador-like slashes, the top of the tree begins to vibrate and several large branches come crashing down, two of them within inches of the chainsaw operators working down below.

"We had a guy get killed by a falling branch a few months ago," Cameron says. "Worst thing I ever seen next to Blake floating facedown in that river slough."

"You saw her?"

"They wouldn't let us get close, but a few of us rode over on our boat to see."

Eventually, the immense oak comes crashing down, striking the ground with an enormous earth-shaking thud, landing with surgical precision exactly where the crew wanted it to.

I am in awe of what I've just witnessed, and we are quiet a few more moments.

I think about how much work was involved in bringing down that big tree and how effortlessly Michael had felled tens of millions of trees in a morning.

"Everybody loved Blake," he says eventually. "I'm not just saying that because she's dead, the way some people do. Nobody wanted her dead. Nobody wanted to hurt her. She was just so damn nice and sweet and good. Not even assholes like Brody and Kieran would want to kill her. People say one of them may have tried to rape her, but I'll tell you this . . . She told me—we were talking about a girl we knew who got raped, and she said she would never fight or struggle, no matter what. She would lay there and do exactly what the rapist told her to do. And she meant it. She . . . I just don't think what happened to her was the result of a fight. I really don't. The sex would-n't've bothered her enough to get into a—"

"Not all rape is about unwanted and forcible sex," I say. "For some rapists, violence, brutality, and murder are the main reasons."

"Yeah, I just don't see those guys like that. Maybe they are, but if they are, wouldn't they have done it before or since?"

"Chances are," I say. "And we intend to find out."

"I know you've heard the rumors that she and I met up that night or that she snuck out to come see me," he says, "but I never saw her. As much as I wanted to see her . . . I can't bear the thought that she got herself killed coming to see me. And I don't think she did. I think Bri may've said something like that when they couldn't find her—just wondering where she might be."

"Unless she already knew and was trying to deflect suspicion onto you."

"Wouldn't put it past her," he says. "But if she didn't have anything to do with what happened to her and she really didn't know where she was . . . I've always hoped Blake said something to her about me or wanting me back or even wanting to sneak out to come see me that caused Bri to say what she did."

"Where was the houseboat y'all were staying in that night?" I ask.

"Second to the end closest to the Barge Bar," he says.

"So only a quarter mile from where Blake was camping," I say.

He nods. "Yeah. Why?"

"That means it was also a quarter mile from the slough where she was found," I say.

"Yeah?"

"And, unlike the campsite, you were upstream," I say. "So if her body went into the water near your houseboat, it could've floated to where it was found."

15

I'm sitting in my truck outside Otis Washington's place waiting for Nash, thinking about my conversations with Cameron and Hailey Perry, as NPR news drifts in and swirls quietly around me.

Otis Washington is an old blues guitarist recently retired from the road, who graciously gives Nash guitar lessons two afternoons a week.

I'm second-guessing something I said to Cameron before leaving the house in Honeyville—not because of what I said but because of the potential it has to shut down future conversations.

I had turned to leave—even taken a few steps away—but turned around and called him back over to me.

"It's none of my business and I wasn't going to say anything, and I know people don't usually take unsolicited advice, but . . ."

"Huh?"

"Your wife," I say. "She deserves better."

He narrows his eyes and clinches his fists and sticks out his chest as he takes another step toward me. "Better than what?"

"Being an *also-ran*," I say. "Always coming in second to someone who didn't even run the race."

"Oh," he says, the tension in his body deflating some.

"She's smart and insightful and sensitive," I say. "Nothing's getting past her, so it's hurting her even more than it would certain other types of people."

"I know," he says. "I do. I just don't know what to do about it. I care about her. I do. Feel like shit for . . . feeling the way I do. Tell me what to do."

"You've got to exorcise the ghost," I say. "Lay Blake to rest."

"You don't think I've tried?" he says.

"You don't have to try to let go," I say. "You either let go or you don't. And if you don't it's because you're still holding on, not really letting go."

I can tell he's thinking about it.

"You told me you didn't want to see a psychologist because you didn't want to not think of Blake every day. That's not letting go. That's holding on."

"Yeah, I guess it is."

"You're holding on to a wish, a desire, a fantasy," I say. "Something you never had and never can. And it's making you and your wife miserable."

He drops his head, takes a deep breath, and lets it out in a long, low sigh. After a few moments, he looks up at me, his eyes glistening.

"Can I come talk to you sometime?" he asks. "Maybe bring Hailey?"

"Absolutely."

I hear something and am pulled out of my thoughts. I look up to see that Merrill has pulled up next to me and rolled down his window.

I roll mine down.

"Whatcha you stakin' out Otis for?"

"He's giving Nash a lesson," I say.

"In guitar?" he says. "Boy already knows enough about the blues."

I nod. "No question. How're things with you?"

He shrugs. "You know . . ."

Recently, Merrill had become an investigator in Dad's department, and his transition into the position and the politics and bureaucracy of a paramilitary-type organization haven't gone smoothly.

"Things any better with the job?" I ask.

He shrugs again. "Some. Sometimes. Maybe. It may just not be for me."

Merrill and I have the same position—only in different counties. He's in Potter in my dad's department, and I'm in Gulf in Reggie Summers's department. I think about how many times I've come close to walking away—or being asked to— since I had been a sheriff's investigator, and I can only imagine how much more difficult it has been for Merrill to stay.

Right now his primary reason for staying is the opportunity he sees to combat institutional and systemic racism and his desire to close the first case he caught after taking the job.

"Any movement on the case?"

I recall standing in the middle of Main Street in the middle of the night, just outside the pool of bright light illuminating the shocking crime scene, the flashing lights of patrol cars bookending the cordon at each end of the block. And at the center of it all, a black man hanging from a noose around a large limb spreading out over Main Street from one of Pottersville's oldest and largest live oak trees.

At the time, Merrill wasn't sure he could work such a case. Since then, it had been his primary focus and at times the only thing keeping him from turning in his resignation.

He shakes his head and frowns. "Not much. What you working on?"

I tell him.

"So it's one of ours?" he says.

"Yeah," I say. "I'd appreciate you taking a look at it and see what you think."

He nods. "Plan to."

"Just be discreet," I say. "Dad made it clear he considers it closed and asked me not to reopen it."

"Seriously?"

"Serious enough to refuse to let me see the file."

"I'll see what I can do about that."

"Don't do anything to—"

"To what? Risk a job I'm not sure I want?"

16

W hen I crawl into bed later that night, I find Anna reading through the binder on Blake's case.

Behind her reading glasses, which make her look even more intelligent and sexier, her eyes are moist, and the glasses rise on her nose as she sniffles occasionally.

"That poor child," she says. "And her mother."

"You mean *Kat*?" I say.

"And those assholes that did it," she says. "I'm as mad at them as I am upset for Blake and Kathryn."

"We don't know for sure they did it," I say.

"They did it," she says. "They're responsible for what happened to her—even if it's not directly, and I suspect it is. They should've never had her up there. They should've never been up there."

I can tell that her lawyer's mind is working.

As usual, the sanctuary of our bedroom is cool and dim and peaceful, the box fan providing a breezy barrier against the world outside this one.

"She has a wrongful death case to make," she says.

"She's brought one."

"Good. Tell her I'd be happy to help with it if she needs any."

"I will. Thank you. That's very—"

"Have they started taking depositions? Can you get me what she has so far?"

Her concentration is complete, her focus on the file total.

"I'll see what I can do."

I glance at the binder and see that she has read farther in it than I have.

"Is this all you have so far?" she asks, tilting her head down to indicate the binder.

"And all I'm likely to have," I say.

She looks up, her eyebrows raised. "Why's that?"

"Sheriff doesn't want to share it with me."

She looks confused and glances back down at the binder, flipping through the pages. "I thought— Didn't Potter County take the lead?"

"They did."

She looks back up at me. "Your dad is refusing to give you a copy of the file?"

I nod.

"Why's that?"

"I'm not sure exactly," I say. "Says it's closed, that it was an accidental death, and he doesn't need any bad publicity to come up during the campaign."

She shakes her head. "After all you've done for him . . . I can't believe he would . . . That really pisses me off, John. All the cases you've solved for him. All the ways you've been there for him."

It's sweet of her to be angry and offended on my behalf—so sweet, in fact, that I don't mention that she wasn't a fan of me reinvestigating this case either.

"Couldn't Merrill get it for you?" she asks.

"He offered, but I hate putting him in that position."

"I have so many questions," she says.

"Let's hear them. I won't have any answers because you're farther in the binder than I've gotten, but it'll help me to—"

"I'm sorry for how I acted about you investigating this case," she says. "I feel bad for how I behaved. It was just insecurity. I love you so much that sometimes I get . . . I'm just . . . I want to protect what we have."

"I should've talked to you before I ever went over there," I say. "And I should've called you back sooner while I was there."

"My heart breaks for Kathryn," she says, shaking her head. "I just keep thinking what if that was one of ours. I want to help with this in any way I can."

"Start by asking me your questions," I say. "Sharing your conclusions with me. And then take a look at the wrongful death suit once we get a copy of it."

"Why didn't Blake's boyfriend—what was his name? Trevor. Why didn't he go to River Fest with her?"

"I plan to ask him."

"What's the deal with Elon DeVaughn?"

"Who?"

"Brody and Kieran's friend who helped them set up the camp Friday afternoon," she says.

"Haven't heard of him. Is that his real name?"

"He helped them set up the camp Friday afternoon before Bri and Blake arrived. One of the witness statements mentions him. Says the three guys spent the afternoon acting like fools on jet skis, but then he's not mentioned again. Did he camp up there too? Did he camp somewhere else or leave for some reason? I did a quick search for him online. He seems as sketchy and sociopathic as Brody. Maybe more so. He's older than the others and seems to have a lot of money."

"Didn't know he existed," I say. "I'll track him down."

"What about Blake hitting her head?" she says. "Do we

know how bad it was? Did it really knock her out? Did it contribute to or cause her death?"

In some of the reports it's mentioned that Blake hit her head on a tree or rock in the water while rope swing diving on Saturday morning.

"Plan to find out," I say. "All the witnesses said she acted fine all of Saturday afternoon and night. She's seen on some of the video footage dancing and cutting up with her friends. But we need to find out for sure."

"I'd really like to see a copy of the autopsy report," she says. "It's alluded to a few times as being sloppy, scant on details, and incomplete, like the rest of the investigation, but it's not in here."

"Yeah, we need to see it," I say. "Hopefully, we'll figure out a way to."

"I can file FOIA for you, but it won't be quick and there's no guarantee they'll turn over everything you need."

FOIA, or the Freedom of Information Act, gives the public the right to request access to records from any federal agency. Since 1967, federal agencies are required to disclose any information requested under FOIA unless it falls under one of nine exemptions that protect interests such as personal privacy, national security, and information pertinent to open law enforcement investigations. State, county, and local governmental agencies have their own versions of FOIA. Anna is using the term FOIA generically because the request she would file would be with the Potter County Sheriff's Department and not the federal government. Potter County, like all Florida counties, falls under the Florida State Sunshine Laws, which go even further than their federal FOIA counterparts.

"You'd think on a closed case ruled as accidental there would be no reason to hold back anything."

"You would," she says. "But your dad is holding the entire file back for some reason."

"It feels odd to be on the outside of a case again," I say. "It has been a while. Dad having the file and refusing to share it with me makes it even stranger."

"There's something else . . ." Anna says, and I can hear the hesitance in her voice. "I've been putting off asking you. I . . . I don't want to ask it, but I have to."

"Okay," I say. "What is it?"

"The timing," she says. "In looking at everything . . . Blake's age . . . Kathryn would've had to have gotten pregnant around the time you were with her. So . . . I have to ask . . . Is she yours? Scott was Kathryn's father's name, right?"

"Right," I say. "Father Thomas. Kennedy is just Kathryn's pen name."

"*Well*?" she says.

"I don't know," I say. "I asked Kathryn who the father was. I'd assumed it was Steve Taylor, but I wondered the same thing you did when I looked at her age."

Kathryn and I weren't involved for long, so the likelihood of me being Blake's father is small, but given the timing it seems like it is at least possible.

When I went to St. Ann's after the second breakup of my marriage to Susan, I wasn't in a good way. Not only had my life been poisoned by violence and alcohol again, but Susan, who had gotten pregnant during our reconciliation, had decided not to have our child. My affair with Kathryn had been brief but intense, and though my attraction to and longing for her persisted for a while after I returned to my life, I never contacted her again. After a few years it faded, but it never went away. During those intervening years I came close to calling her a few times, but I had given Steve Taylor my word that I wouldn't, and I didn't. I did see Susan again—a few times, in fact, which is how Johanna was conceived, but I resisted the temptation to break my word and contact Kathryn. Now I wonder how different my life would be if I had—or if Kathryn had reached out to me. I have already gone through the painful experience of finding out I had a daughter who had been kept from me once, and that was only for four years. I can't even begin to take in that it could be happening again—over a much, much longer period of time and only discovering it after she has died.

"What did she say?"

"She said she would tell me soon, but was too upset to get into it when I asked her," I say. "She's very fragile and has been through so much . . . I haven't pressed her on it. Not that I've spoken to her much since I asked her. But I plan to bring it up again the next time I see her."

"It's . . . Either way it's unfair to you not to tell you."

"How does it make you feel?" I ask. "Even the possibility she might have been."

"Makes me feel a lot of different things," she says. "Makes me angry with Kathryn that she asked you to start the investigation without knowing if it's your daughter's death you're looking into. Makes me even sadder and . . . upset about her death—especially if she was yours and you never even knew about her. And that also makes me angry with Kathryn too—if she didn't tell you all this time. And, of course, it's hurtful. It brings up your relationship with her, which already gives me issues and insecurities, and potentially connects you to her in a very deep and profound way."

"I'm sorry," I say. "I'll try to get her to tell me tomorrow and I'll let you know as soon as I do."

"I know it doesn't change anything," she says. "Not for our relationship, not for how you'll investigate the case, but it would have to make you feel—well, *you* tell *me*. How will it make you feel if she was yours?"

"I'm already so saddened by what happened," I say. "Feel so bad for Blake and Kathryn, but . . . if she was mine and I never got the chance to even meet her . . . I've been trying not to think about it because it will be devastating. I'll grieve for her in an entirely different and deeper way, and I'll be angrier at Kathryn for keeping her from me than I can say."

"Yeah," she says with a wry little wisp of a smile, "that's the only upside I can see."

I laugh and the atmosphere around us lightens a bit.

"I did have the thought . . ." she says. "Thinking about how I would feel if she was yours—do you see Chris when you look at Taylor?"

"Never," I say. "I see you and me and Johanna and John Paul, and now Nash and our family. I never see him. Do you see Susan when you look at Johanna?"

She shakes her head. "It's the same for me. I only see her and us."

17

"**I** can't even begin to imagine what you've been through or how you feel," I say.

Kathryn and I are on opposite sides of a weathered wooden picnic table down by the lake at St. Ann's. I had found her here writing when I arrived, and now her closed laptop sits on her notebook and file folders on the seat beside her.

The peaceful early morning has a soft, airy quality, the ascending sun permeating everything with peach and coral, the still surface of the lake mirroring the delicate pastel brilliance of the sky.

"As far as I'm concerned, you've been through the very worst thing that can happen to a person," I continue, "and that means you're entitled to all the leeway and free passes in the world. But . . . before we go any further . . . I need to know who Blake's father is."

"Do we have to do this now?"

As she grows distressed, the smooth, pale skin of her face begins to resemble cracked porcelain, and her eyes take on a frightened little girl quality.

"I think we need to," I say. "*I need to.*"

"You're not going to like the answer," she says.

That must mean that Blake was mine. I will only not like the answer if she kept my daughter from me for all those years.

"And I . . ." she continues, "I need your help with the case."

"I won't stop helping you with the case," I say. "No matter what."

I wonder what she thinks she could possibly say that would make me quit the case. If she tells me Blake belonged to someone else, nothing changes. If she tells me she was mine, she's got to know that if anything I'll work even harder to find out what really happened to my daughter.

"And honestly . . ." she says, "I'm not sure I can bear you being mad at me."

When I had been here all those years ago, when Kathryn and I had been together, I shared with her that part of the reason I was here was to heal from the second and final failure of my marriage and Susan terminating her pregnancy. She knew how devastating I found that, how badly I wanted to be a father—knowledge that would make her betrayal all the more cruel.

"What if I give you my word I won't stop investigating?" I say. "No matter what your answer is. And what if I tell you that no matter what I feel about what you say, I'll do my best to keep it to myself."

"I feel so . . . I'm embarrassed and ashamed and feel so guilty and also kind of ridiculous and silly."

"Why?" I say. "Why would you feel all those things?"

"Because . . ."

"Because why?" I say. "Kathryn, come on. Just tell me."

"Because . . . I honestly don't know," she says. "As . . . absurd and improbable as that sounds . . . I swear to you it's the truth."

"How can you not know?"

"You *know* how," she says. "After you and I had our . . . little . . . fling . . . I tried to make things work with Steve. That's what everyone seemed to want or feel was expected—Sister Abigail, you—"

"*Me?*"

"You left me and never came back."

"That's not what happened," I say. "I was here on retreat. That retreat ended and I returned to my life. We talked about it before I left. We talked on the phone a few times in the weeks after I was back home. You had already moved on, were already with Steve."

Ignoring what I said, she says, "If Blake came a little late she's yours and if she came just a little early she's his, but . . . by the time she arrived, Steve and I were . . . well, we weren't anything and I knew we never would be. And you . . . I knew you were hung up on Anna and always would be. I didn't want him and I couldn't have you . . . But I had her and that was more than enough. Remember, I was raised as an orphan. All I ever wanted was to belong to someone and have them utterly and completely belong to me. I left the father's name blank on the birth certificate and gave her Father Tom's last name. I let Steve think she was yours and never even let you know about her and . . . It was wrong to all three of you, but I didn't care. I wanted what I wanted and . . . It was the most selfish thing I've ever done in my entire life. I'm so sorry. I truly am. I had been—I had hoped I'd never have to have this conversation with anyone. When Blake would bring it up I'd beg her to trust me and not pursue it. She always had, but I could tell that wasn't going to last much longer. I always wanted it to be you, but I didn't really want to know whose she was because as long as I didn't, she was just mine. She only belonged to me and I only belonged to her."

I think about all she has said.

"Say something," she says. "Please."

"Can I have a minute to process it?" I say.

"No," she says with a small smile.

I do my best not to think about the betrayal to Blake, Steve, and me. I try to put myself in Kathryn's place, in her position with her experiences, and I try to breathe slowly, remain calm, and not overreact.

"I understand why you did what you did," I say. "Especially given your childhood experiences. I empathize with you, and I'm glad you had her all to yourself for as long as you did."

I think about how kind and loving and radiant everyone says Blake was, and wonder if perhaps she had been conceived on that spring afternoon in the woods not far from here when Kathryn and I had our transcendent spiritual and sexual experience.

"But?" she says.

"But . . ." I say. "It was spectacularly unfair to Blake, not to mention Steve and me."

"Are you— How angry are you with me?"

"I told you I wouldn't express how I felt after you told me, and I won't."

"I want you to."

"No, you don't," I say, and it comes out in a manner I didn't intend.

"So you are furious. I knew you would—"

"I'm honestly not saying or expressing how I feel," I say. "All I'm saying is that I'm not going to. I gave you my word and I'm not going to break that. You didn't want me to express anything before you told me and you don't really want to change that now, even though in this moment you think you do. I've told you that I understand why you did what you did. Let that be enough. And leave it at that."

"Okay," she says with a sigh. "I will. But know this—I know what I did was wrong. And I'm truly sorry. Truly. To all three of you. But right now I'm apologizing to you. I know I have wronged you and I'm asking you to forgive me."

18

"How are you?" Anna asks. "Are you okay? Tell me what you're feeling. I still can't believe she did that. Can you come home?"

"I'm okay," I say. "I'm . . . I'm feeling a lot of different emotions, having a ton of different thoughts, but I'm trying to set them aside temporarily. I'm on my way to an interview with a Pine County investigator. I just wanted to let you know as soon as I did."

"I can't decide what's worse," she says. "Not telling you, not having the tests done, not telling Blake, or telling you now."

"She said she knows how unfair this is and that she had no plans to ever tell me, and wouldn't have now if I hadn't asked. Said she hesitated a long time in asking for my help with the investigation because she feared this might come up."

"John, I love you so much," Anna says. "And I'm so sorry you're having to go through this. I wish you could come home."

"I keep looking at her picture," I say. "Keep trying to see some of me in her. Keep wondering what might have . . . How her life would've been if I had been in it, been there for her.

What mine would've been like with her in it. I keep thinking there's no way she would've been in the situation she was in if she were mine and I was in her life."

"I can picture her calling you," Anna says. "Telling you the situation she was in and you showing up a few hours later with a houseboat for her to stay in. And you and Merrill taking Brody and Kieran for a little walk in the woods."

My eyes sting and a smile spreads across my face as I listen to her.

"You're such a great dad, John," she says. "Our children are so lucky to have you. If the world were a better place, every child would have a dad like you. Which would make the world a better place. Regardless of who her father was, I wish Blake could've had you in her life. Like Taylor and John Paul and Nash. As wrong as what she did to you is, it's her daughter that she really robbed."

I try to take in everything she's saying and don't respond right away.

"Tell me what I can do," she says. "How I can help."

"You're doing it," I say. "Your support and kindness are exactly what I need right now."

"Please come home as soon as you can so I can do more," she says. "And call me after the interview to let me know how you are. Okay?"

"I will. Thanks."

I pull over on the side of the rural highway I'm on, park the truck, turn on the flashers, and take a moment to process, to rage, to grieve.

My anger at Kathryn and the sense of betrayal I feel at what she has done is only exceeded by my grief for Blake and the obsessive wondering of what might have been.

Is it possible I had a daughter who died before I even got the chance to meet her? If so, what do I do with that? How do I deal with it? How do I keep from letting it take me down? I can see how easy it would be to spiral out of control into a black hole of regret and rage and grief and obsession.

Could I have saved her? Could my presence in her life have caused her to be a different person—one who would never be up on that cliff with those people? Could my love and nurturance and encouragement and acceptance have caused her to be more secure, more stable, more peaceful, less willing to compromise, less willing to be treated poorly, less likely to ever be around people like Bri and Brody and Kieran?

My phone vibrates. I have no plans to answer it until I see that it is Merrill.

"You okay?" he asks. "Anna told me to call you and check on you. What's up?"

I take a deep breath, let it out in a long, low sigh, and tell him.

"Well . . . *fuck*," he says.

"Uh huh," I say.

"That's . . ." he says, then, "*Fuuuck*."

"That about sums it up," I say.

"What can I do?" he says.

"You already have. Thanks for calling to check on me."

"You up for a little unsolicited advice?"

"You have an open solicitation," I say.

"I know you. I know how that big brain of yours works. Always got to be running on something, working on it, always needin' a problem to solve. Why not open one of those big boxes you have in the basement and put this in it, lock it up—at least for now. At least until you know for sure. Not like you gonna work the case any differently no matter who her daddy is, so . . . lock it away and put all your effort and energy on this."

"I will," I say.

"Sooner the better," he says.

"I know. Already started trying to drag it down to the basement."

"Holla if I can help," he says. "I mean it. Don't wait until you're down a bottomless rabbit hole."

"I won't."

"We both know that's not true," he says. "So *I won't let you.* I'll be bothering you, checking on you and shit for the next several days, so just go on and get used to it."

"Thanks."

"It's funny," he says. "I always merge Susan's two pregnancies in my mind. Associate Johanna with the Justin Menge case, but—"

"Me too," I say. "I think we all do."

After returning home from my retreat at St. Ann's back then, things were better for a while, but that didn't last long. During several years of being single and dating some, Susan and I saw each other some too. I never pretended it was anything other than what it was—clinging to someone familiar during dark nights of the soul. On one of those occasions she got pregnant, but unlike the previous time, she never told me. I probably still wouldn't know if I hadn't discovered her on my own. During that period of time, I worked fewer cases and put most of my focus on being an effective prison chaplain, but the few homicides I did investigate are among the darkest I ever have, most of which I've never talked with anyone about.

"I know why you do it," he says. "Try to block how many times you and Susan hooked up after it was supposed to be over for good."

"Never been too good at turnin' off the faucet so it doesn't drip."

"No, you ain't," he says. "But they's also some other things from that time you tryin' to block out too."

"No doubt."

"Well, do the same with this," he says. "Lock it up for now. Work the case. Spend extra time with the sixteen kids you and Anna raising like your own, don't get anyone else pregnant in the meantime, and . . . holla at your boy if you need anything."

19

I arrive at Dixie Landing before Thad Jones. After finding a place to park, I pull out my phone. I've missed several texts from Kathryn.

I really am sorry. Please forgive me.

Looking back now, I can't believe how selfish I was, but at the time it all made sense to me. Clearly, I wasn't thinking clearly. I'm so sorry.

Please don't stop trying to find out what happened to Blake. Please. Even if you never want to see me again. Do it for her.

I emailed you an article I found that's not in the binder I gave you. At least I don't think it is.

Please respond.

After reading all the texts, I respond: *I will never stop. You know that. I'll touch base with you this afternoon to let you know how today goes.*

Closing my text app, I open my email and read the article she sent.

. . .

New Witnesses Give New Details about Defendant in Blake Scott's Wrongful Death Suit

TALLAHASSEE, FL — Brody Oakes, Bri Allen, and Kieran McClellan were camping with 21-year-old Blake Scott at a cliffside campsite on the Apalachicola River in Potter County over Labor Day weekend in 2015. The next morning she was missing, and later that afternoon she was found dead in the river.

The Potter County Sheriff's Office ruled the death accidental, suggesting she fell from the cliff. The medical examiner who performed the autopsy mentioned blunt trauma consistent with a fall and possible drowning, and pointed out that Blake Scott was intoxicated.

But the case was not that simple. Her family filed a wrongful death lawsuit in December 2016.

For starters, an off-duty Pine County sheriff's deputy on the scene did not believe it was an accident. Not for a moment.

His doubt began the moment her body was found, when he says Kieran McClellan and Brody Oakes immediately appeared.

"On the way out there, I saw the two boys in a canoe hanging onto a houseboat just waiting, directly looking at where the body was," Dawson Lightner said. "When we come back, they started screaming 'Our friend is missing, our friend's missing.' It seemed staged."

When the deputies started asking questions, things got even stranger.

"Spending time with Brody and Kieran, I could definitely tell something was wrong there," Lightner said. "The way they lawyered up. The way Oakes said, 'Let me do the talking.' Their demeanor—no remorse. They weren't saddened by the loss of their friend. They were scared. They had the wrong body language."

Now two new witnesses have come forward, including Brody Oakes's ex-girlfriend, who says the Potter County investigator at the time was not interested in what she had to say about Brody's past.

"I told him start-to-finish what I knew, and I even told him Brody did have a violent past and that's why we broke up," Claire DeGarmo said. "He said that has nothing to do with it, there is no violence in this matter, it was an accident and we are trying to prove it was an accident."

DeGarmo was interviewed by law enforcement because the evening before Blake went missing she'd had an altercation with Bri Allen over their dating history with Brody Oakes.

The fight on the deck of the Barge Bar made the police report but nothing about Brody's past did.

Claire DeGarmo said she even showed the detective pictures of her previous injuries—bite marks, bruises, even one on her neck—and talked about the night he was arrested.

"He lunged at me, was mouthing 'I hate you,' just kinda like calling me things," DeGarmo said. "Then he got into his cell and was hitting the glass, flicking me off, telling me he hated me," DeGarmo said.

None of that, by the way, is in the Potter County investigative report. DeGarmo said the whole interview ended with a warning.

"The investigator even said before I walked away, 'Things always get crazy with a death, even accidental ones. You'll be safe if you talk to me, but if you talk to anybody else I can't protect you,'" DeGarmo said. "He tried to scare me."

The family always felt the investigation was rushed and sloppy.

The 911 calls made that day are missing. When Scott's mom Kathryn Kennedy asked for her belongings, the Potter County Sheriff's Office told her it didn't have them.

"Sleeping bag, clothes, flip-flops, most of what she brought —they had no idea," Kennedy said.

The family hired a private investigator who went to great

lengths to demonstrate that although the cliff is steep, it is impossible to get to the water. It is on a slope with trees, bushes, rocks, even pathways. If she did fall in, where is the evidence?

"Police have said she fell off the cliff, but exactly where did they say she fell?" Private Investigator Frida Price said. "Show me the pictures of the blood on the rocks. Show me the broken twigs."

Price said they had seven people look over the case, veteran investigators, and all seven have the same questions.

Since our earlier stories were printed, a witness named Don Richards has also come forward. Richards is the owner of the Barge Bar, the floating entertainment epicenter of River Fest.

"Right at midnight I was shocked to see a white male swimming toward the dock," Richards said. "I saw this young man climb up on the dock of the barge. The young man appeared extremely distraught and worn out. He was spitting up water for several minutes. The young man told us that he had almost drowned when he swam from the area of the bluff to the marina dock."

Richards believes he saw Oakes the night of Scott's death.

"I am sure that Oakes is the young man that came up out of the water that night," Richards said.

He also reported what he saw to law enforcement.

"I called the Potter County Sheriff's Office to report what I had seen," Richards said. "The Potter County Sheriff's Office advised me that if it became of interest, they would contact me back. I never was contacted again by their office."

This statement directly contradicts what Brody Oakes told police about that night, that they were all in bed at the campsite by two that morning.

Despite all this, the case is closed.

20

My phone vibrates and I pull it out and look at it.
It's Merrill.

"You got that shit locked in a box yet?" he asks.

"For now."

"Good. What program y'all use for records?" he asks.

"SmartCOP," I say.

"Us too."

SmartCOP is a software product for law enforcement agencies that includes computer-aided dispatch, records management, and a variety of other functions used throughout our department.

"All files for the last few years are in it and mostly online," he says. "We still got some paper files too, but not many."

Most everything, including audio and video recordings, witness statements, autopsy reports and the like are stored digitally in SmartCOP, which is backed up in about four different places around the country. Sometimes there are physical file folders with corresponding case numbers, but just as often everything is in SmartCop and can be printed out if a print copy is needed.

"Thing is, and I just learned this," he says, "every time anyone in the department accesses a file it is logged. So I take a look at a case—like, say, the Blake Scott one, the sheriff and everybody else will know I did."

"Yeah," I say, "and we don't want that."

"No, sir, we do not," he says. "Fortunately for us, Blake's case is old enough that it's not in SmartCOP. Before the department switched over to SmartCop, it used something called Code 3 or something like that. Anyway, it's not nearly as sophisticated and doesn't include many options, so there's a lot in the physical files for those cases. Accessing the online files in Code 3 isn't logged like it is in SmartCOP. Only if you edit or print anything, so—"

"No, but with the help of IT someone could go in and find out if you accessed it if they wanted to."

"True," he says. "So I'm gonna access a bunch of old files. Blake's will be one of many, and I ain't gonna print anything. So . . . occasionally I just gonna call and tell you shit. Like today."

"Thank you, Merrill," I say. "I really appreciate it, but I don't want you jeopardizing your new position for—"

"Not up to you," he says. "This what I got for you today. The autopsy report reads like it was written by the sheriff's department instead of the ME's office. Matches perfectly with all of Jasper Wallace's conclusions and even editorializes a little bit. Wallace's investigation ruled Blake's death accidental, suggesting it was the result of a drunken fall off the cliff. And guess what? Medical examiner says in his autopsy report that the blunt force trauma to Blake's head was consistent with a fall, that she could've died from it or drowning—even though he notes there is little to no water in her lungs. And then he actually includes in the report that she was intoxicated."

"Tox results say anything else?" I ask. "I keep hearing that Brody and Kieran had a lot of drugs up on the cliff that weekend."

"Nothing in her system but alcohol," he says. "She was twice the legal limit."

"He draw any conclusions about the lack of water in her lungs or her body not sinking?" I ask.

"None."

When I end the call with Merrill, I say, "Hey, Siri, call Sandy Lewis."

Sandy is a retired forensic pathologist I worked with in Atlanta. I often call her when I have forensics questions because she has forgotten more than most pathologist will ever know—and she takes my calls.

Sandy doesn't have a cell phone, so when Siri says, "Calling Sandy Lewis Home," she's being far more literal than she usually is.

Christy, Sandy's wife, answers the phone.

"Hey, John," she says. "I'm so glad you called. This quarantine is driving us crazy. It'll do Sandy good to talk to someone besides me—especially about forensics. She's bored out of her gourd."

"When the pandemic is over y'all need to come to Florida for a visit," I say. "We'd love to have you and you need to meet Nash."

"Sounds divine," she says. "Let me grab San. Take good care of yourself, John. Stay safe."

"You too."

Since Sandy detests small talk, I only briefly ask after her health and dive right into the case. I give her some background and the pertinent details and launch into my questions.

"I've always thought that dead bodies sink initially and only float later when the gasses of decomposition cause the body to rise, but Blake had only been in the water for a relatively short time—fourteen hours at most and maybe significantly less. Yet she was found floating facedown."

"Most corpses do sink," she says. "There are a lot of variables and factors in how long they stay down, but most definitely sink. And yet some bodies don't. And the truth is, we don't know why. Maybe it's more body fat. May be air trapped in the clothing. Swifter currents. But the truth is . . . we really don't know."

"So there's nothing necessarily suspicious about her body being found floating so soon after death?" I ask.

"Not in and of itself."

"What about cause of death?" I say. "The ME mentions the blunt force trauma to her head. Some of the witnesses say that the victim hit her head on a rock or a log earlier in the day on Saturday. But everyone agrees she seemed fine afterwards—all afternoon and night on Saturday. Could she have sustained a blow to her head and seemed absolutely fine for fourteen to twenty hours or so and then suddenly die from the blow?"

"Absolutely," she says. "This happens not infrequently. It's the reason your mother wouldn't let you go to sleep after you banged your head. It's called a delayed intracranial bleed and it is usually in the form of a subdural hematoma. The trauma will damage some blood vessels that will leak very slowly. It can take many hours for death to occur. Sometimes days. Occasionally weeks. Depends on how long it takes before the blood accumulates to the point to cause problems. And though these types of injuries can sometimes be delayed many days or weeks, typically if the bleeding is going to be severe it'll be delayed only a few hours. The person usually is a little confused after the hit, as anyone would be, but then they clear up. They feel better except for maybe a mild headache, but they are awake and alert and thinking clearly. We call this the lucid period. Then the level of consciousness will begin to decline and the person will slip into a coma and without medical intervention can easily die."

"That's very helpful, thanks," I say.

"Just pay me in the usual way and don't skimp."

My usual method of payment involves shipping her jars of tupelo honey.

"You got it," I say. "So what about the ME saying it's possible the cause of death was drowning even though she had little or no water in her lungs?"

"The diagnosis of drowning is a very difficult one—mainly because water seeps into the lungs passively even if the person is dead after being tossed in the water. This means that finding lungs filled with water doesn't necessarily mean drowning. The ME will look for signs that the victim actually inhaled the water rather than it seeping in passively. This is usually done by looking for damage to the nasal passages from straining to take in air when there is none. She will also look for debris from the water deep in the sinuses and in the lungs. If these are found, it likely means the victim breathed in the water rather than the water passively entering the lungs. In this case, with little to no water in the lungs, drowning probably could've been conclusively ruled out as cause of death. I'm not sure why it wasn't."

"Leave some leeway," I say, "to help cover up a sloppy investigation."

"It's possible," she says. "I'd never do anything like that, and I wouldn't accuse another ME of doing it without a good reason, but, as I say, I can't think of a good reason why it's in there the way it is."

"The autopsy doesn't include an estimated time of death," I say. "That's unusual, isn't it?"

"Highly," she says. "The three most important things the medical examiner must determine are the cause, the manner, and the estimated time of death. Virtually all autopsy reports contain all three."

21

T had Jones is a soft-spoken, early thirties black man with a gentle manner. He's an investigator for the Pine County Sheriff's Department and was the first investigator on the scene when Blake was found.

He is late arriving at the landing, which is fine. I was able to make good use of the extra time.

"Sorry I'm late," he says.

"I appreciate you meeting with me," I say.

"It's no problem," he says. "Hope I can help."

Dixie Landing is Pine County's biggest and busiest public landing on the Apalachicola River. We are both parked beneath the sparse shade of a couple of planted palm trees near the playground and are leaning on our vehicles as we talk.

Like Merrill is in Potter County, Thad is my equivalent in Pine County, though he's much younger than me and Merrill, and wasn't much older than Blake and her companions when he began the investigation into her death.

"I got a lot of respect for you and Merrill," he's saying. "I hope to be half the investigators y'all are one day. 'Course

Merrill says you're the very best. I know I don't have the talent you have."

"Like everything else," I say, "talent is the least of it."

"Then what?"

"Study, practice, lack of ego, openness, feedback, consistency," I say. "Mostly just hard-ass work."

"Well, I'm doing that," he says.

"Then it will pay off."

"Hope so. You ready to take a boat ride?"

I nod.

He leads me down to the floating dock and the boat that is moored there. We get in and he drives us upriver to the slough where Blake's body had been found.

As we near the slough, I look across the river at the bluff where the four kids had camped that weekend, and then slightly farther upriver to the Barge Bar bobbing up and down on its anchor.

Everything looks slightly different from this angle and perspective, but the cliff still looks dangerous and deadly and like the last place anyone should camp.

Thad eases off the throttle, the bow of the boat dropping back down into the water, then angles us in toward the slough and cuts the engine, letting us drift the rest of the way in.

"I've always felt bad about this case," he says. "I thought it was just an accidental drowning at first too, but as soon as Dawson Lightner came up and told me what he did and as soon as he saw the way those boys were acting—"

"Brody and Kieran?"

"Yeah. Came up here when no one was supposed to even know there was a body here, talkin' 'bout 'Is that our missing friend?' You mean the one you never reported missing? The one you never searched for? That friend? Then the way they acted in the boat when I arrived and had Dawson take them back over to the barge."

According to Dawson, both Brody and Kieran were acting suspicious, and on the boat ride back to the barge, Kieran started freaking out.

"When Dawson caught Kieran staring at him and asked what he was thinking, Kieran responded, 'I'm thinkin' how I can get that gun away from you and get off this fuckin' boat,'" Thad says. "Dawson said Brody told Kieran to settle down and not to say anything. 'Stick to the story. Let me do the talkin',' he said. When I asked him later what he meant, he just said he meant stick to the truth."

The boat has drifted about ten feet or so into the slough and stops as the bow bumps into a fallen cypress tree that extends across the twenty-foot width of the tributary.

"This is where she was found," Thad says. "But not on this side of the log like you'd expect. On the other side."

I look at the fallen tree again.

The bank on the right side where the upturned root system is exposed is higher than the bank on the left side where the top of the tree lies. Over half of the thick tree's four-foot circumference is underwater everywhere but on the right side near the bank.

"That always bothered me," Thad says. "Her body would have to float over to that one small spot on the right for it to even be able to get to the other side. Unless . . . it was deep enough under the water to actually float under the log, but the slough is shallow and if the body was submerged, chances are it'd get hung up on something underneath. Not only is there only a few feet between the log and the bottom of the slough, but there's all kinds of other debris in there—other limbs and bushes, trash, old fishing line. You know how the river is."

"And if her body was submerged," I say, "and somehow did pass beneath the tree, it wouldn't have resurfaced so quickly on the other side."

He nods vigorously. "Exactly," he says. "There were no signs of bloating. That body did not sink and then rise later. There wasn't enough time."

"So it's far more likely that someone placed Blake's dead body in the water on the other side of the tree than that she floated there," I say.

"And that's just once she was in the slough," he says. "That's not even factoring in that there's no way her body would float across the entire river without being seen and without drifting downstream."

I nod. "True. You're a very good investigator."

"Didn't get to be on this case," he says. "I was just about to shift gears and work it more like a homicide, but then we were told that Potter County had jurisdiction since the body was presumed to go into the water over there, and they were taking over. I told Jasper about Dawson's and my suspicions, but he showed nothing but disdain for me. Not only was I young and inexperienced, but I was black. For someone like him . . . a person doesn't get much more disregardable than that."

I smile.

"What is it?" he asks.

"Makes me happy that he's working for Merrill now."

He gives me a smile of his own. "Hadn't thought of that. But yeah, that's all right. Bet his bigoted little ass is fit to be tied."

"Before Dawson said what he did and the boys acted the way they did," I say, "you didn't suspect foul play?"

"Wasn't closed to it," he says. "Hadn't reached any hard and fast conclusions yet, but . . . body floating facedown in the water . . . no obvious signs of trauma . . . your first thought is drowning. Hadn't factored in the floating across stream and how difficult it'd be for the body to get on the other side of the tree yet."

"You didn't see any signs of trauma?" I ask. "Nothing on her head?"

He shakes his head. "Couldn't see much. Her clothes were

covering what little of her shoulders and back were showing and her hair hid most of her head."

"Did you notice her clothes?" I ask.

"Not really. Potter took over before I got a chance to do much of anything. I've heard her mom said the clothes she was in weren't hers. I feel so bad for the mother. Over the years, as I learned more about the case, I became even more convinced she didn't get justice, and I hate that some of my mistakes early in the case may by the reason."

"That kind of openness and lack of ego and questioning is what makes a great investigator," I say.

"I've never understood Jasper's response," he says. "Or Potter's entire department for that reason. Not sayin' anything bad about your dad. I know he's a good sheriff and the majority of what's gone on in the case has been while Glenn was in office."

"I don't agree with how they've handled it—and that includes Dad's handling of it," I say. "So feel free to speak freely."

He shrugs. "Don't have much to say about the matter . . .'cept makes it seem like they've got something to hide."

"Yes, it does."

I glance back over my shoulder toward the cliff on the other side of the river.

"Did anyone mention at the time it being suspicious that her body was supposed to have floated over the current of the river into a slough nearly straight across from the campsite?" I ask.

He shakes his head. "No one mentioned where her body went into the water," he says. "Certainly not that they thought it was over there. Didn't know it was until we were told it was Potter County's case. But I'm still not convinced that's where her body went into the water—whether it was a homicide or not. It can't be. I mean, I know there are strange, unexplainable things in suspicious deaths all the time, but that one just seems impossible."

"Did you stick around after Potter took over?" I ask.

He nods. "For a while, yeah. I've never seen such sloppy, inept, incompetent police work in my life. It was hard to watch —even from a distance. It was late on a Sunday evening when they came in, and the sheriff was out of town and Jasper must have been on call, and guess what? Jasper had been drinking. I could smell it on him. It was obvious to everyone he didn't want to be here. He concluded right away that it was an accidental drowning without even pretending to investigate. Just wanted to wrap it up and get back to his Labor Day party or something. They pulled her body out of the water and into the boat without any equipment and without a body bag, just laid it in the bottom of the boat. Didn't even have a sheet to place over it. Eventually someone threw a hoodie or something over her upper body. Contaminated any evidence there was—not that they were going to look for any anyway. Didn't take any pictures, measurements, nothing—not body temp, not water temp. Didn't even wait for the ME investigator to get here. First time the ME's office even saw the body was on the dock at Potter Landing. Now, I think the ME made some mistakes in the case, but . . . the body and any evidence it may have contained was way compromised before the ME even had a chance to get started. Jasper didn't keep the suspects separated or get proper statements. And he let them take a deputy up to the campsite to get Blake's things. No crime scene techs, not even an investigator. A deputy with the suspects. 'Course he didn't consider them suspects, so . . . The deputy snapped a few pics with his phone up there, and they are the only ones we have of Blake's belongings and the possible crime scene. The deputy comes down without Brody and Kieran, and evidently without Blake's things because they were never logged into evidence and her mother never got them back. A few minutes later, everyone in the area can see a big campfire up there on that cliff. What the hell were Brody and Kieran burning? Blake's things? Evidence? Their drugs? Later that night the three of them—Bri, Brody, and Kieran—gave statements at the station. They were treated like traumatized witnesses, not suspects. And that's what passed for an investigation in this case."

22

When I get back in my truck and check my phone, I see that Merrill has sent me crime scene and autopsy photos.

Even before I begin to study them, I forward them to Sandy Lewis. I then open each one, enlarge it, and examine it carefully.

Each image is a picture of a picture, snapped with Merrill's cell phone camera. Odd lighting and reflections further compromise the already low-quality images, but not so much that they aren't useful.

In one image, taken from a boat, Blake's body can be seen floating facedown in the slough, shoulders hunched, arms out, hands down, hair sticking to her head and splayed out on the surface of the water around her, loose T-shirt revealing a twisted bathing suit strap beneath, a pop of pink from the bright neon athletic shorts sideways on her bottom.

Another image shows Blake's phone, keys, flip-flops, and a few random clothes on the ground just outside a tent on the cliff.

Another reveals her purplish-pink torso and the marks and

abrasions it bears. By far the most disturbing is what looks to be a bite mark on her abdomen and a triangular-shaped impression on her solar plexus.

How could anyone, particularly an investigator and medical examiner, look at those and not consider foul play was involved?

The biggest takeaway from the other images of her body is how relatively few scratches, abrasions, contusions, and other marks and signs there were that she fell and then rolled through the various trees and branches and bushes and rocks and vines and thorns to crash onto and injure her head on a rocky outcropping on the cliff or in the water below. There is significant damage to be sure—particularly to her head, but nothing like I'd expect to see from such a long, fatal fall.

I'm still looking at the images when Merrill calls.

"You see that shit?" he says.

"Looking at them now."

"Is that a bite mark on her torso?"

"Looks like it," I say.

"And the hell's that triangular mark?"

"No idea. Never seen anything like that. But it's certainly suspicious."

"What I thought," he says.

"Even more suspicious that there's no mention of either one in the autopsy report," I say.

"Exactly," he says. "Same true of the marks on her neck and the trauma to her throat."

"Haven't gotten to that yet," I say.

I place him on speaker and tap back over to the pictures, scrolling until I find the photos of Blake's neck.

"Looks like she was choked or strangled or at least started to be," he says, "and they's no mention of it in either the investigator's or the ME's reports."

I think about what Claire DeGarmo said about how Brody Oakes liked to choke her during sex.

The photos of Blake's neck show a faint purplish pattern that could be handprints.

"What's worse," he adds, "the autopsy reveals severe hemorrhaging of her larynx, but it ain't even noted in the autopsy report. Not so much as a mention."

As I scan through the other images, I encounter two photos of her thighs. The inside of each thigh shows bruising in configurations I've seen before—in sexual assault cases where the victim's legs were forced apart and held open by the knees of the attacker.

Two other images show what looks like handprints on her biceps, as if she had been grabbed violently and held forcibly.

The next photo shows Blake's nose, which appears bloody and broken, and her mouth, the top lip of which is split on the right side.

"What they put that poor girl through before they killed her," Merrill says.

"I know," I say.

"Hard to imagine a case can be made now with how inept the original investigation was," he says, "without them preserving evidence. With the investigator and the ME just focusing on anything that might possibly back up their theory and ignoring the mountain of evidence that contradicts it."

Every image I see makes me think it far more likely her injuries were the result of assault instead of an accidental fall.

"Yeah," I say. "I'll be interested to see what Sandy Lewis says about them."

"Point is . . ." he says. "If they's a need to go off the reservation on this one . . . I'm yo huckleberry."

"Okay, Doc," I say. "I'll keep that in mind."

"Do," he says. "'Cause I'm sick to fuckin' death of entitled punk-ass little frat boy bitches doin' what the hell they want with impunity."

"I second that emotion," I say, closing the photos and taking him off speaker.

"You think Jasper really that incompetent?" he says. "Or had another reason to whiff that shit so bad?"

"You're his co-worker," I say. "You tell me."

"Haven't seen anything makes me think he's that incompetent," he says. "They say he got a drinkin' problem, but that didn't keep your white ass from becomin' the spiritual lovechild of the celibate detectives Brown and Holmes."

23

After finishing with Merrill and before leaving the landing, I check my voicemails. I have one from Kathryn.

"I know you said you'd call me when you could, but . . . I couldn't wait. Please call me back. I need to talk to you. Need to explain myself better. Need to apologize again. Anyway . . . Okay. Call me back. Please. Soon as you can. Oh, and I emailed you another article I think you'll find interesting. You may already have it. I have so many documents I can't keep up."

I open my email and read the article.

POTTER COUNTY SHERIFF'S Investigator Admits He didn't Llisten to 911 calls, Order a Rape Kit, or Search for DNA Evidence

Incompetent neophyte investigator looking into the mysterious death of a woman admits shocking lapses in the investigation before ruling the death accidental.

Potter County Sheriff's Investigator Jasper Wallace was

deposed in June 2018 as part of a civil lawsuit in the 2015 death of Blake Scott.

Scott, 21, was camping with three friends when she was found floating facedown in the Apalachicola River in Florida on the afternoon of September 6, 2015.

After a two-month probe, Wallace officially concluded that Scott fell into the river and either died from the fall or drowned.

His report detailing his findings was just three paragraphs long.

Wallace acknowledged he had never worked a homicide before and had no special training to do so.

The investigator said he did not listen to the 911 calls reporting Scott's death, nor did he speak to the callers or other potential witnesses.

He also failed to look for blood at the campsite, did not swab Scott's nails for DNA evidence, and didn't order a rape kit because she was on her period.

None of the friends on the camping trip were ever charged with any wrongdoing in connection to Scott's death.

Scott's mother, author Kathryn Kennedy, has used her savings to hire a private investigator, Frida Price, in an effort to find out what really happened to her daughter.

Kennedy was not satisfied with the results of Wallace's probe and in 2016 filed a $10 million wrongful death lawsuit against her late daughter's friends who had accompanied her that weekend—Brody Oakes, Bri Allen, and Kieran McClellan.

The friends always denied any involvement in Scott's death.

As part of that lawsuit, Kennedy's lawyers deposed Detective Wallace, forcing him to detail his investigation into Scott's death, revealing the gaping holes in the case.

When asked why he did not talk to the 911 callers, Wallace replied, "I just didn't."

The investigator also said he did not know when Scott was

last seen alive and he did not attempt to speak to the residents of houseboats that were docked not far from the spot where her body was discovered by fishermen.

When asked if he looked for blood evidence on the rocks at the campsite, he replied with a bowed head, "No, not specifically, no."

Potter County Sheriff Jack Jordan conceded in July 2018 that Detective Wallace could have collected more information.

Scott's family hired a hydrologist who determined that if the young woman fell from the cliff where she and her friends were camping, like Wallace's report stated, it would have been impossible for her body to float against the current to the slough across the river where it was found.

During the deposition, Wallace admitted that he did not factor in the direction of the current during his investigation and did not think to bring in a diver to look for evidence in the river.

"I didn't. I just didn't," he said.

After watching the recording of Wallace's deposition, Scott's mother said she was shocked by his answers. Others present the night of the death agreed.

"There is no way that was an accident. I will go to the grave believing that girl was killed, her body was moved, and they are hiding the truth," Dawson Lightner said.

Lightner was an off-duty deputy providing security for the River Fest event.

Scott's friends told police they were all drunk when they returned to the campsite and Scott fell asleep in a hammock close to the cliff edge.

When they woke up the following morning, they said Scott was nowhere to be found and they assumed she had gone off to meet someone.

Scott's friend Bri Allen did tell police she was worried because Scott's clothes, flip-flops, phone, and wallet were still at the campsite. Allen said she went looking for her friend, presuming she would run into her at the event.

But Frida Price, the family's private investigator, claimed autopsy photos show a strange bite mark near the young woman's breast and that Scott had bleeding in her throat, suggesting strangulation.

"There was nothing accidental about this death," Price said. "And me and my team are going to prove it."

24

"I feel like I failed her," Frida Price is saying. "I surely do. But . . . God as my witness, I took that case as far as I possibly could. Maybe the legendary John Jordan can take it further—maybe even all the way home. Wouldn't that be nice."

Frida Price is a short, round, older black lady who lives by the framed cross-stitched motto that hangs on the wall behind her desk: Do No Harm. Take No Shit.

We are in her small, old, cluttered office on MLK in Panama City not far from Bay Medical Center, which is still undergoing repairs from damage done by Hurricane Michael.

A PI since the 1970s, it appears Frida hasn't changed her wardrobe, office furniture, or decor since then. And based on the dusty stacks of file folders and three-ring binders, I'd say she's never thrown anything out during that time either.

Sitting across from her now, it hits me who she reminds me of. Frida Price bears an uncanny resemblance to Russell Cosby, the smallest and youngest member of the junkyard gang from the Fat Albert cartoon I watched as a kid. She's roughly the same size and shape, and like him she dresses like it's winter regardless of how hot the Florida summer actually is. And though she's not wearing them now, the old wooden coat rack in the corner holds several earth-tone scarfs and blue and purple Russian-style ushanka hats complete with fur linings and ear flaps.

"I tell you . . . God as my witness, I wanted to get a better result for her—the mom," Frida is saying, "but the investigation was so fundamentally flawed from the beginning . . . Not like I could go back and process the crime scene or have a proper autopsy conducted, including a rape kit. 'Bout the only thing I could do was gather new witness statements, and not much of nobody would talk to me. Hope you can do better, but to be honest I doubt it. Ain't sayin' you won't come up with a good theory—hell, we all done that—but you won't be able to prove it. No evidence to prove it with was ever collected. 'Cause no real investigation was ever done. Tell you what . . . I've got a copy of my report around here somewhere. Why don't you read over it while I make a phone call, then I'll answer any questions you have?"

"Sounds good to me. Thanks."

It takes her a while, but eventually she locates a few sheets of wrinkled paper containing an actual typewritten report.

After donning a gold scarf and blue ushanka, she steps outside into the ninety-plus degree heat to make her call, and I begin reading her report.

Much of it is already familiar, so I scan the pages, stopping occasionally to read certain paragraphs more closely, trying to glean anything new. I'm most interested by her final conclusions:

I strongly disagree with the official findings and believe a thorough investigation was never conducted.

When I reexamined the autopsy, I discovered the original investigation failed to disclose that Blake had hemorrhaging in her throat, which could have indicated choking. I was also mortified to find out that a rape kit was never performed because, as the sheriff's investigator explained, Blake was on her period and had a tampon in and so couldn't have had sex.

Blake couldn't have fallen from the cliff and landed in the water and her body couldn't have floated over across the flowing stream of the river to wind up in the slough where it was discovered.

During Blake's autopsy, lividity was noted as being evident on her chest, and the ME was able to make out a distinct triangle shape. This indicates that Blake's chest had to have been pressing against something shaped like a triangle for a significant period of time after her death. This was never even attempted to be explained by the original investigators.

This investigator believes the most likely scenario is one of three possibilities:

One. Something happened once the four arrived back at the campsite, Blake died, and the three friends decide to dump her body in the slough to make it look like she fell from the cliff.

Two. Bri and/or Brody were directly involved in Blake's death. Bri attacked Blake. A fight ensued. The guys got involved and Blake was killed in the struggle.

Three. I must acknowledge that it is at least possible, though highly unlikely, that Blake's death was a genuine accident such as an alcohol-related illness or injury, but they panicked upon finding her body and decided to dispose of it so as to avoid any trouble.

All three of these scenarios would require significant efforts on behalf of the suspects to get Blake's body back down and into the water while they were heavily inebriated. But because of the remote location of the camp and the large amount of time between their return to camp and her body being found the next day, and with no determined time of death, this could have happened anytime over a number of hours.

In conclusion, this investigator strongly suspects that, though the three so-called friends were involved in and responsible for Blake's death, the original investigation is so fundamentally flawed that there is no evidence to support my suspicions. Unless someone confesses or becomes willing to provide evidence on someone else, I'm afraid that this case will remain officially an accidental death in which authorities partially blame the victim.

I LOOK up from the report.

"Questions?" Frida asks.

She is back at her desk, still wearing her gold scarf and blue ushanka hat, and looks even more like Russel Cosby than before.

"The obvious one," I say. "What's not in the report?"

"That the mom wanted to keep payin' me to work on it, but I knew I'd just be taking her money. Not sure what you plan to do, but with no evidence and none of the principle players willing to talk, what can you do?"

"I plan to just keep taking her money," I say.

She smiles. "She already told me you were an old friend doin' a favor when she called to set up this meeting."

"After your investigation and the conclusions you drew in your report," I say, "does any part of you think it's possible it really was just a horrible accident?"

She nods. "Sure. But it's a very small part. I've done this long enough to know there's plenty of shit in this world that can't be explained. I think it bein' an accident is harder to explain than it bein' foul play, but don't think it impossible."

I think about it.

She says, "You read their statements or listened to their interview recordings yet?"

"Hope to tonight," I say.

"Pay extra close attention to Bri's," she says. "I think if one of them is actually innocent and truly clueless about all that's going on, it's her. Ain't sayin' she is. Just that it might be possible. You listen to it and form your own opinion. She seems naive and clueless, but I could just be showin' my own bias from a lifetime of foolishly overestimating seemingly silly young white girls. Found out the hard way most of 'em ain't playin' dumb after all."

nna and I are sitting on our back patio, holding hands, drinking wine, and watching the sun set beyond the pines on the far side of the lake.

We are enjoying a rare evening alone.

Taylor is playing at a friend's house, and Nash is at Lillian Pritchett's visiting his baby brother Harley.

Lillian adopted Harley when we adopted Nash, and we're trying to give them as much time together as we can.

We had taken advantage of the empty house and made love before we came out onto the patio. Now we are talking about our days, our children, wonderfully monotonous domestic and household things, and the future as it related to my work, the case she's working on right now, and the case I'm working on right now—all between sips of wine, sweet fruit-scented kisses, and stretches of silence to take in the sunset.

"So much stress and strife in the world," she says.

She's right. The world itself seems sometimes to be coming off its axis—and not just because of the global pandemic, but the political and social unrest, the disrespect and disregard for others, the support of and even celebration of the rude and hateful, unkind and untrue, the attacks on truth and trust and the principles of fairness and democracy and the institutions that preserve it, and the natural disasters wreaking havoc on the planet.

"And yet," she continues, "it's so peaceful right here right now, I wouldn't believe all that other stuff is going on in the outside world if I didn't know it was."

"Lot to be said for small-town, slow-paced, family-centric life," I say.

"*An awful lot,*" she says, taking my hand again. "Particularly when you get to live it with the love of your life best friend."

We fall silent again, enjoying the evening, each other, and the wine.

As much as I relish small-town life and as fortunate as I feel to be living the life I am, I'm not unaware of all the suffering and despair many of our neighbors are experiencing all around us—the poverty, alcohol and drug addiction, domestic violence, bigotry, racism, the injustice, the sexism.

After a while she says, "Want me to read the witness statements to you? You're gonna think I'm making them up."

I nod. "I wish you could read all the reports to me while we sit together watching the sun set over our lake for an evening."

"This is Kieran McClellan's," she says. "No joke. It's a copy of a messily handwritten statement, but I can make out most of it. 'Last night the girl came to our campsite for a few minutes saying she was going back to her ex-boyfriend she hung out very shortly then I fell asleep I woke up and she was gone I guess to get together with her ex. She maybe to see this morning and she said she came back after we left and was trying to get with him last night after we seen her at the campsite and she said she was trying to make out with him in front of his new girlfriend to make her jealous and win him back.' And that's it. That's the statement of a twenty- two-year-old college student. That's what Jasper let him get away with. The others aren't much better. Should I continue?"

"I guess, but I feel like my IQ is dropping just listening to it, and I hate to associate your lovely voice with that drivel."

"This is Bri Allen's," she says. "'Last night we was at the Barge Bar we got into the canoes to go home (the camp on the cliff)'—"

"Does she actually write *canoes*, plural?" I ask.

"Actually, I read it that way," she says, "because she wrote *canoes* but then scratched out the *s*."

"Very interesting," I say. "Please continue."

"'We got to the top and all went to lay down for bed and when we woke up this morning Blake was gone but all of her stuff was still on the campsite we thought she might be down at River Fest but was surprised she didn't take her stuff. She wasn't there we immediately went to the campsite we're coming back to the Barge Bar she wasn't up there still but her stuff still was. I went to see if she might have been at the Barge Bar and saw policeman were headed to our campsite.'"

"Frida Price thinks if any of the three are innocent, it's her."

"I've had that thought listening to her interviews," she says. "Interested to see what you think. Of course, she did assault Claire on the deck of the Barge just because Brody flirted with her."

"Why don't you do that when women flirt with me?" I ask.

"I do," she says. "But like Bri, I take them outside. I'm too much of a lady to do it in front of everyone."

"You and Bri are nothing if not genteel."

"And now for Brody's brief masterpiece," she says. "'Blake I saw last when we was canoeing back from the Barge Bar with our group she had cried about her ex-boyfriend who she saw. The next morning had said she tried to make a move on him and he refused said he last saw her going to the houseboat was last seen by me and would say around midnight before Bri and I went to bed in our tent at the campsite.'"

"Wow," I say.

"I don't know who did what to Blake," she says, "but they all murdered the English language. Must have gone to one of those schools that teach punctuation is optional. Thoughts?"

"About optional punctuation?" I ask. "The murder of the English language? The twilight of America? What?"

"Let's start with the statements," she says.

"The boys were both pushing the 'going to see the ex-boyfriend' hard."

"Yes, they were," she says. "And yet Bri didn't mention it. I'm convinced more than ever that Blake was killed and there's a cover-up, but if it's just one of them or even two . . . How are you ever going to be able to prove it?"

26

L ater that night, lying in bed next to Anna as she sleeps, I listen to an audio recording of Bri Allen through my AirPods.

The first recording was done by Dawson Lightner on his cell phone shortly after Blake's body was discovered in the slough.

They are on the noisy deck of the Barge Bar and the phone is in his shirt pocket, so the recording isn't great, but I can make out most of what is said.

"Where'd y'all sleep or where were y'all last night?" Dawson asks.

"Up there," Bri says in a soft, teary voice.

She must point to the bluff.

"Up on that cliff?" Dawson asks.

"Yes, sir."

"Who all? Your boyfriend and the other guy and Blake?"

"Yeah," she says. "Everybody was up there."

She sounds genuinely upset.

"Y'all all went up there together?" he asks.

"Yeah."

"And that was at two o'clock?"

"When you talked to her on the dock last night," she says. "That's when we went back up there."

"Yeah. Okay. And what's this ex-boyfriend she ran into or whatever?"

"Well, yeah, but he has a new girlfriend and has nothing to do with it," she says. "And Blake has a new boyfriend. This has nothing to do with any of that. I don't think they even spoke. I don't know."

"Your boyfriend said she tried to talk to him or something," he says. "Did she try to kiss him in front of his new girlfriend and—"

"I don't think so," she says. "But—not that I know of. She may have confronted him or— She's full of drama. Wouldn't put it past her, but . . . I don't know for sure. I know it—this—has . . . whatever this is has nothing to do with him or her. Them, I mean."

No one else has accused Blake of being dramatic or confrontational.

"What do you mean?"

"I don't know. I just . . . Cam's a good guy. He's got nothin' to do with anything. Blake broke up with him. I think . . . I'm pretty sure he'd take her back in a heartbeat."

"Okay. How many of y'all slept up there last night?"

"Four."

"You, your boyfriend, the other dude with the long blond hair, and Blake?"

"Yeah. Yes, sir."

"Y'all canoed over to the camp together?"

"Yes, sir."

"And she was fine?"

"We had all been drinking, but yeah. We just crashed. Been a long day. And when I woke up this morning she was gone. I asked Kieran—he was in a hammock—where she was. He said, 'She's not in the tent with y'all?' I said, 'No, she was never in the tent with us.' He said, 'I don't know then. Haven't seen her.'"

"Did y'all go anywhere after you left the bar?" he asks. "Another camp? A houseboat?"

"No, no sir. Straight up there and crashed. Ex— We were exhausted from the day and we had been drinking and it was late. Just wanted to crash. Everybody . . . Kieran was trashed. We had to get him from another boat before we left here, had to help him. We were all . . . Nobody felt like doing anything."

"What do you think happened?"

Bri begins to cry. "I know she probably went to pee, but . . . she didn't have her shoes or keys, wallet, phone—and she would, like, not leave without that. So . . . I don't know. I just . . . I can't understand. You know? Like, I know . . . I've known her since we were ten. I know she wouldn't leave without that stuff."

"EMS and Potter County Sheriff is over there now," he says. "They'll figure out what happened and—"

"I thought . . . I did think, maybe she did go somewhere to hook up with someone or see her ex-boyfriend or hang out with her . . . with her other friends. She was, you know, popular, and had a lot of friends. Maybe last night. Maybe this morning before we got up."

"But you said she left all her things?"

"Yeah," she says, "yeah, you're . . . I did. I just . . . I'm just trying to—"

"And you said she was wiped out and too tired and drunk to do anything."

"Yeah, well, yes, sir. She was."

"Did she say anything about doing anything else or going to see her ex or—"

"No, no, I'm not sayin' . . . I just . . . I'm just tryin' to . . . I don't know."

She starts crying again, louder this time.

"Why did this have to happen?" she says. "Why do bad things always happen to me? I'm so tired of . . . Why does everything have to be so hard, you know? Just for once . . . Why can't we have a nice time with no drama?"

She breaks down again.

"Take some deep breaths," Dawson says. "Try to settle down. We don't know anything for sure yet."

"Yeah we do. I wouldn't be here talkin' with you if we didn't know."

"What makes you say that?"

"It's pretty obvious. My friend is missing and we can't find her and y'all found a body. And the whole time I've been worried she might have gone to pee and fell, but then I came down here and heard she might have got on a houseboat . . . so I thought she'd be around River Fest today, but . . ."

"Who said she got on a houseboat?" Dawson asks.

"Alex. Well, he said she came back in and said we left her so she'd have to find a houseboat to stay on."

"Why would she have to do that?"

"Because we had canoed back without her. Well, she thought we had, but we had just been over to . . . visiting. She thought we left her, but we had just gone over there. So she told Alex her brother's friend that she wasn't going to have a place to stay."

"Wait, now," Dawson says. "I didn't follow that. Y'all went back to the camp without her?"

"No. She thought we did. She thought we had left her at the bar. So I guess Alex said that she said that because we had left her, she was goin' to have to find a place to stay. But we were just visiting people. And I don't know if that was before or after she last saw me, so . . ."

"Didn't you say y'all went back to the camp together last night and she stayed up there with y'all?"

"Yeah."

"So what she told Alex about the houseboat was prior to you getting back with her and going back to the camp together?"

"Huh? Yeah, I guess. Yeah, yes, sir. She went back up there with us."

27

"Did you count how many different stories she told?" Anna asks softly.

It's early the next morning and we're at the kitchen table having breakfast with Nash and Taylor—and Johanna via Skype.

I've never been much of a breakfast eater, and stopping to eat has never been a part of my morning routine. I used to get up with just enough time to get ready, rushing out the door in time to make it to where I was going, and even though I rarely eat, starting my day here with everyone is one of the best parts of my day.

We've been mostly interacting with the kids, but as they turn to talk to each other, Anna is anxious to know what I thought about Bri's interview.

I nod.

"It's hard to tell sometimes even in person, let alone from an audio recording," I say, "but she seemed genuinely upset."

"Oh, I think she was."

"Question is," I say, "was it because she thought she was caught or because she was truly sad her friend died? And either way, her state of mind could explain how scattered her thought patterns were and the seeming contradictions."

"Could," she says. "But I don't buy it. She wasn't going to correct that bit about the houseboat until Lightner called her on it, made her explain."

"You're probably right," I say.

"If it was an act," I say, "it was masterful. Pretty scary how genuinely sad she seemed and how subtle her subterfuge was."

She checks to make sure the kids are engaged in their own conversation. They are in a deep discussion about what they will do when Johanna is here this weekend.

Anna leans in and whispers behind her hand, "Has Kathryn considered exhuming the body? Given how incomplete the autopsy report was, how inept the investigation."

"I'm not sure," I say. "She hasn't mentioned it. But you're right. It might give us the evidence we need to solve it."

"It'd allow for a paternity test too," she says. "Have you thought about whether you'd like to—"

"*Paternity test,*" Taylor says in a loud and exaggerated manner.

She has heard Anna whispering and keyed in on what she knew she wasn't supposed to hear.

"What is *that*?" she asks.

"Finish your breakfast," Anna says. "We've got to go. Everybody ready to have a great day?"

"It okay if Natalie comes over to study tonight?" Nash asks.

"Study what?" I ask with a smile.

His eyes widen and twinkle a little and he gives me a smile of his own. "Nothin' that will require a paternity test."

"Can we believe anything Bri says?" Kathryn asks.

"I sure as hell don't," Addie says.

"She's a compulsive little liar," Claire says. "How many different stories has she told? How many times has she contradicted herself?"

Kathryn has reached out to Blake's friends for help, and a small group of them have gathered at St. Ann's to answer questions and discuss the case.

Cameron Perry, Blake's ex-boyfriend, is here, but his wife Hailey had to work. Blake's friends Claire DeGarmo and Addie Morrissey are here. As is Addie's little brother Alex. Dawson Lightner said he'd be here, but hasn't shown up yet.

Bri Allen comes up first.

"She told me and a group of at least three other people that all four of them slept in the tent," Addie says.

"I feel bad for her in some ways," Claire says. "She's in a toxic relationship with a frat boy sociopath and she's just trying to survive."

"I still can't believe he married her," Addie says.

"Has to be to keep her quiet," Kathryn says, "right? I mean, he was texting Blake all kinds of flirtatious messages in the weeks leading up to River Fest."

"She wasn't the only one," Claire says. "He kept telling me he wanted us to get back together, acted like we already had. Never once mentioned Bri. I was shocked to see him with her at River Fest."

"Why's that?" I ask.

"He and I had always been on again off again," she says. "I was stupid enough to keep taking him back. He'd come to me crying, saying he couldn't live without me, that if I didn't take him back and take care of him he'd kill himself. I really thought I could change him. Anyway, after he put me in the hospital, my family and friends forbade me from seeing him, so we'd sneak around some. And when we did, he'd say he was seeing so and so but it was just for a cover for us, she didn't mean anything to him, that kind of thing. He never once mentioned Bri. Not once. He showed up at my dorm room Thursday night."

"The night before River Fest?" Kathryn asks.

"Yeah. Even spent the night. I mean, we had sex Friday morning, and he never once mentioned taking Bri to River Fest a few hours later. I even said as he was leaving, 'Will I see you at River Fest?' ''Course,' he said. 'You know where I'll be.' He knew I'd never stay up on that cliff again, so I figured he'd stay there and I'd stay on the houseboat and in front of everyone we'd play it cool. Never mentioned Bri. I even texted him from the Barge when I got there that afternoon 'cause I could see a flag I bought him at Thunder Beach flying over the campsite. Told him it looked good and that we needed to go to Thunder Beach again this year, and he wrote back *for sure*. When I asked him what the plan was, he said he'd see me later that night in the bar, and then later that night he walked in with Bri. That tells you everything you need to know about him and their relationship—if you can call it that. Nobody had ever seen them together before that weekend and two months later they're married."

Addie says, "I'm not even sure he intended to hook up with her there. They didn't go together. We know that. I think she sort of forced her way up there, and used Blake to do it."

"What do you mean, *used Blake to do it*?" Kathryn asks.

"Brody wasn't interested in Bri," she says. "I'm not sayin' he wouldn't fuck her given half a chance. He'd fuck anything that was still long enough given half a chance. But he wasn't into her. He said so. And all you have to do is look at the way he treats her. He definitely wouldn't have let her move in and stay up there with them. But he had always had a thing for Blake. I bet you anything, Bri used that. It was obvious Kieran was into her too. Blake was Bri's ticket to get up on the bluff and into Brody's bed."

"I have a question," Claire says tentatively, "but I'm not sure how to . . . I feel funny bringing it up."

Kathryn says, "I keep telling y'all I want to hear everything —every idea, every theory, everything about Blake, no matter how unflattering it might be."

"This isn't bad about Blake," she says. "Not at all. It's just . . . a little embarrassing for me to talk about, but . . . the cops said they didn't think she had sex because she had a tampon in."

"Yeah," Addie says, "most ridiculous shit I ever heard. Has that guy Jasper whatshisname never had a girlfriend?"

"It's absurd," Kathryn says. "They used it as one of their excuses for not ordering a rape kit."

"'Course you can bone on your period," Addie says, "but even if you decide not to go down that, ah, path . . . they's two more options—what, you can't swab them for semen or DNA or whatever either?"

"Yeah," Cameron says. "They're sayin' online in one of the subreddits or somewhere that . . . well that her neck was bruised and that her throat showed signs of trauma . . . like maybe she was . . ."

"Forced to give oral sex," Kathryn says.

"Yeah," he says. "Sorry."

"Don't be. We've got to go over everything. Every possibility."

"Right," Claire says, "but my question is, do we even know for sure if she was on her period?"

"That's a great question," Kathryn says. "I don't think she was. She and I were very close and usually on the same cycle and we always talked about it. Not that we had to. We could always tell when we were . . . having PMS or our period. She definitely wasn't when she left here that Friday, and I don't think she would have started that weekend."

"Why would her killer stick a tampon in her?" Cameron asks. "What would that—"

"Never know why people do many of the things they do," I say. "Especially killers. He could've put something on it to try to destroy or contaminate evidence or he could've thought if she had a tampon in, the investigator wouldn't suspect rape, which turned out to be the case."

"But what I was wondering . . ." Claire says. "My questions is . . . Could they have soaked the tampon in alcohol and put it inside her to make her seem like she was drunk or had been drinking more than she had?"

I shake my head. "It's a good thought, but wouldn't really work. If it did anything at all, it might soak into the tissue right around the tampon."

"I've got a question," Cameron says. "Well, actually my smart wife came up with it. It's just a thought she had. She called it 'wild speculation with no underlying evidence,' but . . . I think it's . . . good and should be looked into."

"What is it?" Kathryn says.

"Has anyone checked Trevor King's alibi?" he says.

Kathryn says, "The officials didn't check anyone's alibis. They didn't do a real investigation. But I bet the PI did."

"Hailey was saying how the boyfriend is always the first one the cops consider when a girl is killed—and with good reason. They're usually the ones who did it. Anyway, we got to talkin' and . . . He was supposed to be having a party, right? And Blake was supposed to be there for it, but she didn't show. He says he just went to bed, but . . . what if he drove up here? He could've found Blake in the hammock with Kieran or doing something with Brody or just lost his temper because she stood him up and was camping with other guys. I don't know, but . . ."

Claire says, "What if . . . You know how Blake was asking if she could stay with other people and said she was going to drive home?"

"She would have if they hadn't hidden her keys," Addie says.

"What if she called or texted Trevor to come get her?" Cameron says. "What if he did? What if they got into a fight and he killed her?"

"Should be easy enough to find out," Kathryn says.

"I'm not sayin' he did it," Cameron says. "I'm not accusing him of . . . anything. I know what it's like to be accused and suspected just because you're the boyfriend or ex-boyfriend, but—and he seems like a real good guy. He really does. From what I can tell . . . he was good to Blake, but . . . I'm just saying—or Hailey is—he should be looked at like I was. Even though he wasn't there—or wasn't supposed to be."

"I've got an interview with him set up for later this afternoon," I say. "I'll ask him. And tell Hailey if she ever wants a job in criminal investigation to give me a call."

Tires crunch on the gravel and everyone turns to see Dawson Lightner coming up the drive in a small, gray Toyota truck.

"Anybody looked at him?" Addie says. "May be innocent

and fatherly and all, but his interest in Blake before and after her death is . . ."

"Unnatural?" Claire says. "Creepy?"

"I's gonna say *intense*, but . . . yeah. I like your words better."

Kathryn glances at me, her expression asking if I'll look into Dawson.

I nod to her, then say to the group, "We're taking a close look at everyone."

29

I feel a certain bittersweet nostalgia as I drive to Potter Correctional Institution to interview Kieran McClellan before meeting Trevor King later in the afternoon, and as I pull into the staff parking lot, my mind is flooded with memories of my time here.

This is where I had my first experiences of prison chaplaincy, where I restored order to my life, where Merrill and I first started working together, and where Anna and I fell in love as adults.

When I left PCI, it was to take a chaplaincy position at Gulf Correctional in Wewa, which also allowed me to work as a sheriff's investigator. After Hurricane Michael took GCI offline, I resigned my part-time chaplaincy position there and have only been working at the sheriff's department since. I miss ministering in an official capacity—a feeling that only heightens and intensifies as I stand at the control room gate of PCI and check my firearm.

"We sure miss you around here, Chaplain," Sergeant Adams says. "Not the same without your soothing presence and smiling face."

To some, like Stacy Adams, I will always be *Chaplain*, no matter what the title on my business card reads.

Though we are speaking through the glass of the control room window and the open metal tray, the warmth of her words come through.

"Thank you," I say, "that's very sweet of you to say. I miss being here."

After I empty my weapon and hand her both it and the clip to secure inside the control room, she informs me that McClellan is waiting for me in the visiting park.

"Do you think I could see Mr. Smith while I'm here?" I say.

Mr. Smith, a wise, world-weary, elderly black man, had been my primary chapel orderly, and I had missed my daily interaction with him since leaving my post here.

"Oh, no," she says, her countenance falling, "I guess you haven't heard. He passed away last week. Caught corona and just couldn't recover."

I'm stunned, and am unable to speak.

"I'm so sorry. I should've called you. I just figured someone else already had."

It's awkward to be having this conversation through the glass of the control room in the front of the prison, but it would've been difficult no matter where and how it was had.

I feel such sorrow, but also regret. I should've stayed in touch with him better than I did. I always intended to write to him, visit him more, but I didn't—and two demanding jobs, many investigations, a growing family, a Cat 5 hurricane, and a global pandemic are just excuses. Throughout everything, I had the same twenty-four hours in each day that I had always had, and what I did with them was the result of my choices.

"I know he asked for you at the end," she says, "but with the . . . you know, virus and all . . . no one was allowed to . . . So sad how everyone dying of that horrible disease is dying alone."

"Can you give me a minute?" I ask, and step away from the

window, retreating to the far side of control room covering, leaning against the pole for support.

I hate that Mr. Smith had to die here—even more so that he had to do it alone. I wish someone would've called me. I would've come to see him, would have quarantined afterward to protect my family, friends, and coworkers.

I take a few moments to mourn, then a few more to gather myself, and then I enter the institution to interview one of the prime suspects in the suspicious death of Blake Scott.

THE YOUNG MAN sitting across the folding table from me is not the same one from the pictures and videos on his social media accounts. No more swooshy blond hair. No more entitled white frat boy attitude. No more adolescent innocence.

The eyes beneath the bad, close-cropped haircut of the man across from me are serious, sad, wary, scared. His countenance, like his head, is downcast, as if bowed by the consequence of his own behavior.

He's in here on charges related to his third DUI in less than a year—a sign he's spiraling out of control, trying to numb the pain and guilt, punishing himself for what he did to Blake?

"I got no problem talkin' to you," he is saying, "'cause I got nothin' to hide. I don't know what happened to that girl or who did it. I just know I didn't. I swear to God I didn't kill her. And that's the truth."

"Take me through the weekend," I say. "Tell me everything you remember."

"We got there early Friday afternoon."

"We?"

"Me and Brody. Met up with Elon—"

"DeVaughn?" I ask.

"Yeah. He's a friend of Brody's. Got a killer houseboat. Got a killer everything. Rich as fuck. He helped us set up the camp. Well, he mostly sat and drank and told us what to do, but . . ."

"Did he camp with y'all?"

"No, why would he? He stayed on his killer houseboat."

"How much time did he spend at the campsite that weekend?"

He shrugs. "Not much. Don't think he ever came back up after helping us Friday afternoon, but I'm not positive. I'm gonna be honest with you—"

"I'd really appreciate that."

"I was pretty fucked-up all weekend. Some shit is pretty blurry, but I know I didn't kill anybody. I'm sure of that."

"So you set up the camp Friday afternoon . . ." I say.

"Yeah, then we went skiing. Then these two girls show up. I didn't know anybody else was camping with us, but then they were, and I was like it's all cool and all. It's Brody's stuff. It's Brody's spot. I was a guest just like the girls. We went to the Barge Bar Friday night and got trashed. Was hoping to get lucky . . . but no such luck. Went back to the camp . . . sometime around midnight or one. I think. I know it was earlier Friday night than Saturday. And we crashed. Got some z's for the next day. Next day got up and played in the water all day."

"Before you get to Saturday," I say. "Who was up on the cliff Friday night?"

"Just us two and the two girls," he says.

"Who slept where?"

"Well, Brody and I sort of worked it out that me and the one girl would have the tent one night and he and the other girl would have it the other night. It was supposed to be Brody and that Bri chick in there Friday night—and they were for a while. Long enough for him to fuck her, but then he came out and told that other chick, Blake, she could sleep in the tent with Bri and he'd stay in a hammock outside with me."

"Are you sure?" I ask.

What he's telling me contradicts other statements given and the official narrative that is out there.

"As I am about anything. I wasn't just drinking. I was on some pills and shit too."

"So you and Brody slept in a hammock beneath the stars and Bri and Blake stayed in the tent on Friday night?"

"Yes, sir. I believe so."

"The same hammock?"

"No."

"How many hammocks were set up?"

He shrugs. "Four or five I think."

"Were y'all expecting more people to stay up there?"

"I wasn't. Don't know what Brody was thinking . . . but it was his—the whole thing was his thing. I was just crashin' with him."

"What did you and Blake do while Brody and Bri were in the tent?"

"Nothin'. Drank some more. Talked."

"About?"

He shrugs. "Just . . . nothin' really. People I guess. The band at the bar that night. River Fest. Can't really remember."

"Were y'all in the same hammock?"

He shakes his head. "We weren't even in a hammock. We were in chairs."

"There's a picture of you and Blake in a hammock—"

"Oh, I know. The infamous hammock pic. That was Friday afternoon. It was nothin.' Bri told Blake to sit there, she wanted to take her pic. I was just sort of there, so I struck a pose."

"Where'd you guys use the bathroom?"

He shrugs. "In the trees."

"Did you see Blake go that night?"

"Yeah. She didn't go far. Girl wasn't bashful. Probably could've seen her if I'd'a looked, but I definitely heard her."

"Anything out of the ordinary happen Friday night?"

He shakes his head again. "No. I mean, not while I was awake. But once I was out, I was out, so . . . don't know after that."

"You and Brody still friends?" I ask.

He shrugs. "Guess. Not really in touch. Find out who your friends are when you get put in here. Or if you even have any."

"Okay, so Saturday . . ."

"Wake up. Get ready. Head down to the party. We skied. Drank. Hung out. Listened to the bands. Swung on the rope at the landing."

"That where Blake hit her head?"

He nods. "I think. Didn't really see it. But she was—it looked like she was out for a minute. Brody jumped in and swam out and got her. So heroic. I think he thought that was gonna get him some. Said he was gonna hit 'em both before the weekend was over."

"Did he?"

"No idea. I mean, I know he did Bri, but . . . not sure about the other girl."

"What about you?" I ask.

He shakes his head. "Sadly, no."

"But you told Deputy Lightner you had sex with Blake."

"Well . . . You know . . . He was saying, like, they're gonna do a rape kit on her and if you boys have been with her or anything you better tell me now. And I was like, *fuck*, I don't think I was. I'm pretty sure—almost positive I wasn't, but . . . I was trashed most of the time. What if we fooled around while I was . . . and I didn't remember? If they do a rape kit and find any of my boys in there . . . So just to cover my ass I said she and I had fucked. But we didn't. Almost positive we didn't. And I guess we didn't 'cause they never said, 'Hey, we found your baby batter inside her.'"

"Your *baby batter*?"

"You know, come, jizz, whatever."

"What else happened on Saturday?"

"Just more of the same all day. Then went to the bar that night. Don't remember much about that. I'm tellin' you . . . I've never been so fucked-up in my entire life—and that's sayin' something. Elon's got some killer-ass drugs."

"What do you remember?"

"Just drinking more and . . . tryin' to find a place to lay down. Went out to our little boat and crashed."

"But it wasn't your boat, was it?"

"What do you mean?"

"You passed out in someone else's boat and they had to move you to the right one when they got ready to leave that night."

"They did?"

"You didn't know?"

"No. I'm tellin' you . . ."

"And y'all didn't have a small boat, but a canoe, right?"

He nods.

"How were you able to climb up the cliff that night?" I ask.

"I wasn't," he says. "I mean, I didn't."

"You weren't on the cliff Saturday night?"

"Not until later," he says. "Fuckers left my drunk ass in the boat. I woke up at some point and climbed up, but not sure what time it was. It was late . . . or early . . . I mean it wasn't . . . the sun wasn't up, but you could tell it wouldn't be long until the sky began to lighten. I don't know. Anyway, I climbed up and crawled into the hammock."

"Where was Blake?"

"No idea."

"She wasn't there?"

"Not out there where I was," he says. "No one was. I figured Brody got his wish and did them both and they were all in the tent, but . . . Now I don't know. I guess she could've already fallen off by then. Hell, it could've been her splashing in the water that woke my ass up. I don't know. I went to sleep. Bri woke me up the next morning saying, 'Where is Blake?' I said, 'Thought she was with you.' Brody said, 'She probably went to bang her ex-boyfriend,' and that was that. We went to River Fest. I was hungover like a motherfucker. And then at some point Brody said, 'Hey, they found a body over in that slough. Let's go see if it's Blake.' And I was like, '*Blake?*' I was shocked he even thought it could be."

30

"So he's saying he wasn't even up there when she was killed?" Kathryn is saying.

I'm sitting in my truck in the PCI employee parking lot. I should be on my way to St. Andrews already, but I'm not ready to leave yet—and it's not just that I'm sad about Mr. Smith. I'm mourning the relentless passage of time as much as his death.

I miss PCI. I miss being a chaplain. I miss working with Anna and Merrill every day. I miss being a younger man.

I can no more stop time or travel backwards in it than hold back the tide, but it's not just that. I'm powerless to even slow it down. Seconds are bleeding out of me like blood leaking from the wound of a fatally shot man, and there's nothing I can do but sit here and watch it ebb out of me.

"Says the last time he saw her was when they walked into the Barge Bar," I say.

"That's a whole new story," she says. "He's never said anything like that before. Do you believe him?"

"Which time? Which story? Which statement?"

"Exactly," she says. "Did he say why he was willing to talk to you? He hasn't been cooperative. The only time he's said anything was during the deposition and he only gave short answers and only to direct questions and only because he was in prison and didn't have a choice."

"Anna made some calls," I say, "and the judge let Kieran's attorney know that if he cooperated with me she would take it into consideration on his prison time and probation."

"That was very nice of her," she says. "Of Anna, I mean. I've always gotten the sense that she doesn't like me, and given what y'all know now . . . I'm assuming you told her."

"She's a very compassionate person," I say, "and her heart breaks for Blake and you. She's been helping me in many ways and is willing to do anything she can."

"That's so . . . Her kindness moves me more than I can say."

"There are a lot of people working on finding out what really happened to Blake and who's responsible. We're gonna get there."

"For the first time I truly believe it."

"Given all the issues with the investigation and the autopsy . . ." I say, trying to ease into a delicate subject. "Have you considered an exhumation and new autopsy?"

"Yeah," she says. "Frida suggested it, but . . . I just can't. I guess . . . I just think I'd rather have to live with not knowing than to do anything else to my poor child."

"I certainly understand."

After we end the call, I take another moment to mourn, to reflect, to long, to grieve. As I do, it begins to rain—random, intermittent splats on my hood and windshield at first, then faster and faster like drumsticks on a snare head popping out a paradiddle.

Eventually I turn on my wipers, and like time itself, move on.

31

"I've never loved any girl like I loved Blake," Trevor King is saying. "And I never will. No matter how long I live. Her friends told me she used to tell them I was the one, but she—*she* was the one. My one and only forever. Never be another."

I don't doubt that he means what he's saying, but his words have an insincere quality to them, as if he's merely saying what he's heard others say or that he's heard himself say them so many times that they've taken on the practiced, rote, shallow attributes of melodrama. A big part of it is the soft, breathy way he's speaking—like someone trying to sound spiritual.

He comes across as a shallow person trying to sound deep, and something about it reminds me of the persona of a certain type of religious leader.

Trevor King is a neo-hippie hipster who makes and sells jewelry and music. He has thick, matted dirty-blond hair, implacable blue eyes, a thick mustache, and a pale face dotted with stubble that runs down his neck and into his frayed teal and charcoal Baja hoodie. Both the pullover poncho and his long, unkempt hair wreak of pot.

Pushing up his left sleeve and turning his arm over, he reveals a tattoo on the bottom side of his forearm that reads *Blake Forever* in black on a bed of red roses, with *Never Be Another* beneath it.

And I'm guessing with that permanently written in his flesh there never will be.

"Why didn't you go with her to River Fest?" I ask.

I am talking to Trevor on a street corner in downtown St. Andrews while he sets up a table of his jewelry and his music equipment. When he's done, he plans to play for tips and try to sell some of his homemade hemp necklaces.

The rain is gone. The sun is back out. But there's a dampness about that refracts the light and gives every surface a certain shimmering sheen.

"Wasn't my thing," he says. "I was a different person back then. Blake's love and losing her transformed me into what I am now. I was down in Gainesville at the time, had already planned a party for that weekend. Typical frat boy fool. Couldn't cancel on my guys. Besides, Blake was supposed to drive down on Saturday evening for it."

The traffic on Beck is sparse but steady, and we're close enough to the street to feel the force of the wind from the passing vehicles, which is occasionally strong enough to knock over some of Trevor's homemade jewelry displays.

"She tell you why she changed her mind?"

"Whatta you mean?"

"Why she didn't drive down like she was supposed to?"

He gives me an odd look. "'Cause she died, brah."

"We believe she died sometime very early on Sunday morning," I say. "But she had to have made the decision not to leave River Fest and drive down to see you on Saturday afternoon."

"Oh, no, not really, that's just the way Blake was. It was cool. She could get into something and flake on something else or bail on something early to do something completely different.

You just had to be flexible. And I didn't mind. I only half expected her anyway. I wasn't as free and flexible then as I am now. Now I just go with the flow, you know, relax and trust the unfolding path. Back then I was more uptight and . . . just more of a cog in the massive machine, man. But . . . I knew if I wanted to be with Blake, I had to let her be her."

"But it has to bother you," I say. "Being stood up."

"Everything bothered me more back then," he says, "but . . . like I say . . . I was more caught up in the big lie of materialism, capitalism, and control."

Thanks to Floriopolis, Little Village, and other venues, this part of St. Andrews is known for arts and music, often hosting festivals and events and featuring live music at the bars, restaurants, and coffee shops, but it appears Trevor isn't a part of anything like that, and I wonder how long he'll be able to play and hawk his wares before he gets shut down.

"Did you know she would be camping with other guys?"

"Wasn't a problem. I was her *one* and she was mine."

"One and only," I say. "Never be another."

"Exactly," he says, nodding vigorously. "You get it, right? I knew her. I knew who she loved. We had a real chill vibe. Or she did. I do now. No cages, just love."

"Did you two have an open relationship?" I ask.

"We had what we had. No labels."

"No cages, no labels," I say, "but were you free to sleep with other people?"

"We were free to do whatever we wanted."

"Did you sleep with other people?"

He shakes his head. "I only wanted her."

"Did she?"

He shrugs. "Don't know. We didn't talk about it much."

"One of the guys camping with her told a cop he had had sex with her. Does that—"

"He's lying and everybody knows it," he says. "Blake hated dudes like him. No way she slept with him. No way."

"He's now saying it was a lie," I say.

"*See?*"

"I just wondered if it would've been okay with you if she had."

"Anything Blake did was okay," he says. "More than okay. It was great. She was an angel. A great person. I had the ultimate trust in her essential, innate goodness. And no matter what . . . I was the *one*."

"Did you guys talk and text any that weekend?"

He shrugs again. "Some. Pretty sketchy cell service there. But we texted some."

"Did she tell you she didn't like camping with Brody, Bri, and Kieran up on that cliff and wanted to stay somewhere else or leave?"

"She said they were douches and like really lame," he says, "and that she might crash with somebody else. God, I wish she had."

"Did she ask you to come get her?"

He stops what he's doing, necklaces dangling from his hand, the ice in his blue eyes melting into small pools he blinks against.

"Yeah," he says, nodding. "But I got it too late. I was too fucked-up to drive. I was asleep when it came through. And I had left my phone somewhere during the party."

I wonder which it is, that he couldn't drive or that he didn't get the message—and if he didn't get it, was it because he was asleep or he left his phone somewhere?

"I don't know," he continues. "I just . . . I . . . If I had only known . . . what was going to happen . . . I'd've driven up and gotten her."

"But you wouldn't even have known to if you didn't get the message until the next morning."

"Huh? Oh, yeah, you're right, but . . . I wish I had just . . . you know . . . before the party, that afternoon . . . just insisted she leave or gone up and gotten her. I'd do it over if I could."

32

"**D**id anyone ever get a copy of Trevor King's cell records?" I ask.

I use my time in the truck driving from St. Andrews to Downtown Panama City to make some calls, starting with Kathryn.

The afternoon sun is big and bright over St. Andrew Bay, and the stately old homes along Beach Drive are mostly repaired and restored following Hurricane Michael.

Squinting against the brilliant dancing sunlight of the bouncing bay, I can see two small sailboats gliding across the surface of the water in the foreground, as beyond them a massive barge is being maneuvered by a tugboat into the Port of Panama City.

"I'm almost certain that Frida did," she says. "I probably have a copy of them somewhere around here and they may even be in the binder I gave you. Why?"

"Want to check out his story—well, stories, and see if any of them can be verified."

"You suspect him?"

"I suspect everyone."

"Including me?"

I laugh. "You're even less likely to have done it than Trevor—"

"On account of neither of us even bein' there?"

"Well, there's that," I say. "Though she could've called either of you for help and something went horribly wrong. Y'all could've snuck up there that night. Him easier than you."

"*Hey, wait a minute,*" she says. "I'm less of a suspect 'cause I'm a girl?"

"A girl of a certain age," I say.

"*Dude,*" she says. "You're just making it worse."

"And you have less of a motive than—"

"I have *no* motive," she says. "But what is his?"

"I'm not sayin' he has one," I say. "Many killers don't—at least not a known or understandable one. But being stood up and finding your girlfriend camping with another guy could give him one. What if he found them doing more than camping?"

"But if he did, whoever was with her would know—Kieran or Brody or all three—and there's no way they'd keep his secret."

"He could've waited until they fell asleep."

"I guess it's possible, but he's all hippie love all the time now."

"He says her death transformed him. Maybe that's why. He's trying to keep his rage in a cage or atone for killing her."

"How many hemp necklaces will *that* take?" she asks.

We are quiet a moment, then she says, "Found it. He gave his cell records to Frida voluntarily. Which is suspicious as hell."

"Yes it is," I say.

"You should already have it, but I'll email it to you just in case."

I end the connection with Kathryn and call Anna.

"How busy are you?" I ask.

Turning onto Harrison, I glance at the clock in the dash-board. I'm early for my meeting with Merrick.

"You caught me at a good time."

"Would you mind taking a look at something for me?"

"Name it."

"Trevor King's phone records and his deposition transcript," I say.

"What am I looking for?" she asks.

I tell her what Trevor told me, then say, "I'd like to know what calls or texts were made and when. Especially the one from Blake asking him to come get her. He said he didn't get it until the next morning."

"Among other things," she says.

"Exactly. That was only one of his stories. I'd also like to know which towers his phone pinged off of—and if any were up here."

"I'm on it," she says. "Of course, he could've left his phone there when he came up here."

"If he did you know what that would mean," I say.

"That it was premeditated," she says.

While I'm talking to Anna, Dad leaves a voicemail for me.

I listen to it when I end the call with her.

"I know you had Merrill access our records," Dad says. "Did you think I wouldn't check? I was . . . You don't know how bad I was hoping that I wouldn't find anything. I said surely John wouldn't do that to his best friend. Wouldn't put him in that position. But some part of me knew you would. I started to say I can't believe you did that to him, but of course I can. I have no problem believing it. But it shows a level of selfishness and disregard for others—for both me and Merrill—that I wasn't sure even you were capable of. I'm as disappointed in you as I have ever been. Now I'm just trying to decide if you cost Merrill his job or not. If you did, I'll let you know so you can be the one to tell him."

With Dad's words still echoing in my head, I park across from Leitz Music, cross Harrison, and walk into the large, historic music store to pick up a new set of strings for Nash. Fifteen minutes later, I walk out with not only a new set of Elixir strings for his acoustic, but his very first electric—a Lake Placid-blue Fender Toronado that he has no idea he's getting, which I had no idea I was getting just a few minutes before.

33

I meet Merrick McKnight at Millie's.

Located in the front east corner of the old Sherman Arcade building on Harrison Avenue in Downtown Panama City, Millie's features great food and live local music, and, the reason we chose it today, outdoor seating.

Merrick and I sit beneath an umbrella at a table in the courtyard between Millie's and the Corner Pocket pool hall, with a great view of the enormous, ancient oaks of McKenzie Park.

Merrick is a friend and my boss Reggie's boyfriend, and also a reporter for the *News Herald* who had covered Blake's case as a stringer back before he accepted his current position.

After we order, what for both of us is a late lunch, he says, "You think Reggie has any chance of winning?"

I shrug. "She's got a *chance*," I say, "but something dramatic would have to happen."

"Like what, her opponent dropping out of the race?"

I nod and smile. "Yeah, something like that."

"Wonder what she'll do," he says. "Hell, what will you do?"

I shrug again. "Have no idea."

"You worried?"

I shake my head. "No," I say. "It'll work out."

"*Seriously*?" he asks.

"Seriously," I say. "Other doors will open, other opportunities will present themselves—for both of us. I'm not saying I don't have my moments of questioning and wondering and maybe sometimes of even worrying, but mostly I trust something else will open up eventually. Always has before."

"Yeah, guess that's true."

"How are Casey and Kevin?" I say, inquiring about his grown children.

"They're good. Your crew? How is it having a teenage son?"

"Great. I absolutely love it."

We are quiet a moment, and I look around.

The Spanish moss draped over the huge, high, long limbs of the oak trees in McKenzie Park undulates in the gentle afternoon breeze blowing off the bay. The sporadic traffic on Harrison passes by slowly, and as usual there's a quiet calm over all of downtown.

"One of the last times I was here," I say, "Dave Lloyd was playing."

Dave Lloyd was a musician and counselor and mutual friend who passed away a few months before Hurricane Michael hit.

He shakes his head. "Still can't believe he's gone," he says with a heavy sigh. "I'm not sayin' it's causally connected, but . . . have you noticed how the world's gone to hell since he died?"

I nod. "I have noticed that."

Our food arrives—a shrimp po' boy for me and a grouper sandwich for him—and our conversation turns to Blake as we eat.

"I'm glad you're on this case," he says. "There's far more to it than the official story. I'm cynical and jaded and believe in most cases the simplest, most obvious answer is usually the truth, but I'll never believe she died accidentally. And no offense . . . but the investigation—if you can call it that—was a joke."

"Why would that offend me?" I say. "I had nothing to—"

"It was your dad's department's case," he says. "And I get it. He had lost the election and was on his way out and some things fell through the cracks. But . . . it says a lot he's willing to reopen it and—"

"He hasn't reopened it and doesn't plan to," I say. "I'm working for Kathryn Kennedy as a—"

"Oh shit, really? Thanksgiving at the Jordans should be interesting this year."

"No doubt," I say. "Tell me why you've drawn the conclusions you have."

"Everybody makes fun of Dawson Lightner and Frida Price throwing that dummy off the cliff," he says, "but I covered it. I was there. There is no way to fall off that cliff and land in the water. It might be possible—for an incredible athlete—to run and jump and maybe make it to the water. Maybe. But no way she went to pee and fell and landed in the water. No way she fell out of a hammock and landed in the water. It's just not possible—not from the cliff, not from the woods on either side. And don't even get me started on them actually saying her body could float straight across that wide-ass river and into that slough—and not just into the slough, but on the other side of that fallen tree. No way. Not possible. And her injuries don't match up with someone falling. She was attacked, maybe even raped. Of course, we'll never know because the idiots didn't order a rape kit. And citing her having a tampon in as the reason is the most absurd thing I think I've never heard a cop say—and I've heard some absurd shit in my time. I'm not an expert, but it looks like she has defensive wounds. It looks like she was beaten—punched in the nose and the lip, grabbed by the arms and neck, choked, and maybe even suffered oral sexual assault. And what the fuck, man, there's a fuckin' bite mark on her stomach and a triangle pattern on her chest. Then you look at the three people she was up there with. They're punks. Criminals. Violent addicts. And I know you can't put a ton of stock in things like this, but look at their behavior following her death. No sympathy. No humanity. No remorse. Kieran posting *best weekend ever*. Brody and Bri marrying and moving. None of them attending the funeral or reaching out to the mom. I get that it looked like an accidental fall and drowning, but just a little investigating would show it wasn't."

I nod and think about it as he takes a few bites of his food.

"You have any theories on who might have killed her?" I ask.

He wipes his mouth, takes a sip of his Diet Coke, and says, "Any of the three of them could have, but I believe it would've taken at least two of them to move the body. But beyond that . . ."

"Any chance it's someone else and not one of the three of them?"

"I think it's most likely them, but . . . if it's not . . . I'd look at that off-duty deputy, Lightner. He's way too keen on the victim and the case. He's still active in it, like maybe he's trying to stay in control of it. The friend who helped them set up the camp but then supposedly didn't stay there. What's his name? Elon DeVaughn? He's a creepy dude. Older than the rest of them. Trust fund playboy. Doesn't seem like the type to even be at River Fest—let alone help set up a camp. And I'll tell you who else is sketchy as fuck. The owner of the Barge Bar, Don . . ."

"Richards?" I offer.

"Yeah, him. He's . . . I don't know what he is exactly, but he ain't straight, ain't legit."

34

"**I**f he ever found out I talked to you," Tasha says, "he'd kill me. Doesn't matter if I told you anything or not. If he thinks I talked about him . . . I'm dead."

Tasha Woods and I are sitting at the bar at the Saltshaker Lounge on Highway 22 in Wewa. It's just before the early drinkers arrive, and we are two of only four people in the place.

The bar is dim and cool and unusually quiet, the alcove with the pool tables and dart board empty.

"He won't hear anything from me," I say.

Tasha Woods was once a bartender at the Barge Bar. She is a thirty-something bottle blond with enormous breasts and thick makeup caked on a face pocked with acne scars. She smells of Dollar Store perfume, cigarette smoke, and alcohol, and her excessive jewelry clinks together from her shaking.

She shakes her head. "I don't know. He'll find out one way or another."

I'm not sure how long she's been here or how many she had before I arrived, but she's got a good buzz going and is beginning to slur her words despite her best efforts not to.

"Just talk to me about you then," I say. "Did you like working there?"

She shrugs. "Not really. It was too . . . much. Too many people. Too much pressure. Too risky. Wasn't for me."

"What was risky about it?"

She shakes her head. "Forget I sssaid that and buy me another drink," she says, getting hung up on the *s* in *said*.

I do the latter.

She drinks her new whiskey sour like it's a shot and signals the bartender for another, her jewelry tinkling with every unsteady movement. The bartender looks at me and I nod.

"Were you working the weekend Blake Scott died?" I ask.

She nods.

"Anything stand out?"

"She was a good girl," she says, slurring her words more often and more heavily. "Friendly. Mannerly. Most of those kids treat you like shit, like their damn slave or somethin'. But she was always polite and respectful. Can't tell you much else. I was working my ass off, slingin' drinks like a mofo. Hardly ever looked up."

"Did she have any altercations with anyone? Did anyone bother her? Was anybody watching her too closely?"

She shrugs. "Not that I saw. Well, maybe . . . I feel bad for sayin' this 'cause he seems like a nice guy, but . . . maybe that cop. The one working security."

"Dawson Lightner?"

She nods. "I think that was his name."

"And it still is. What did he do?"

"I don't know. Like I said . . . I was . . . head down, workin' my ass off. But . . . a few times . . . I don't know. He just seemed a little too into her. Could be nothin'. Ain't sayin' it is. Just tellin' you what I seen, what I thought at the time."

Though no one has fed it, the jukebox comes alive and a B-side Bob Seger song begins to play.

"Did you feel threatened when you worked at the Barge Bar?" I ask.

She purses her lips and shakes her head slightly, her earrings tinkling as she does. "No, not really."

"What was it that made it too risky to do?"

She frowns and sighs. "You're gonna make me tell you, aren't you?"

My guess is the whiskey sours are.

"Well, fuck it then," she says. "Buy me a drink and I'll tell you."

I notice she leaves out the word *another*, but I motion the bartender over and she takes her glass and begins working on the drink.

"And make it a double," Tasha says. "And don't be afraid to put some liquor in it this time."

The Seger song fades and a Tom Petty tune begins to build.

"He gave us the choice," she says. "And don't make me say who *he* is. He would pay us minimum wage and we could keep our tips or . . . he'd give us the product to deal to the customers and we'd make what we made doing that, he'd keep all the sales and tips. It was a good deal. I made a shit-ton more money than I would have if I had just worked for tips, but . . . it was stressful as hell. Trying to keep up with everything, not deal to an undercover cop, not use too much of the product myself. It was a nightmare."

"Did most of the staff do that?"

"All of us."

"Including Lightner?"

She shrugs. "Not sure about him."

"Did he know y'all were?"

"Sure as hell didn't do it in front of him in case he didn't," she says. "So I don't know for sure."

"So Don Richards was operating a floating opium den for kids?" I say.

"I said don't say his name," she says. "But . . . and there wasn't any opium, but yeah, drugs are a big part of why the bar does so well. But that's the least of it. You ever wonder . . . I mean, think about it. The Barge Bar is on a barge, but it's on top of it—just on top, just on the deck. Ever wonder what's below the deck? Biggest fuckin' drug distribution center in the South. Dealers pull up, dock, fill up, and take off with a load of whatever they can sell. And as much of it as they can handle."

35

"**D**o you deal while you're working security on the Barge Bar?" I ask.

"Huh?"

Dawson Lightner and I are standing outside a bar in Mexico Beach owned by Don Richards called Dick's Deep Dive. He's a bouncer here two nights a week.

"Did you not hear the question?"

"Deal what?"

"*Cards*," I say with as much sarcasm as I can muster. "When y'all played canasta, did you ever deal?"

"*What*?" he asks, his voice rising in surprise. "I don't understand."

From inside the building and on an exterior speaker mounted under the far right corner of the eaves, a woman with real pipes is killing a karaoke version of Radiohead's "Creep."

"*Drugs*," I say. "Do you deal drugs? Is that how Don Richards pays you?"

"*No*, I don't deal drugs," he says, looking around us. "And keep your voice down. Why would you even—"

"Have you ever?"

"No, John. I'm not a fuckin' drug dealer."

"Were you aware that other employees were dealing?"

"I'm there to provide security," he says. "Even back when I was a deputy, I was off-duty. I'm not there to investigate. I'm not there to dictate. I'm not there to enforce the law. I'm there to keep everyone secure, keep them safe."

"So you knew?"

"Do I know that some illegal activity happens when that many people are together drinking and partying? Sure. Do I condone it? No."

"I'm not asking you about *some illegal activity*," I say. "I'm asking you about your employer and fellow employees having an organized system for distributing illegal drugs."

"No one told me anything," he says, "but I observed some stuff, yeah."

Across Highway 98, through a vacant lot between two pastel-painted townhouses, the low, orangish moon casts its reflection on the glasslike surface of the Gulf.

"Did you see anyone sell or give Blake anything?" I ask.

He shakes his head. "No, and I would've said something to her if I did. She just drank and she didn't do a ton of that."

"Why would you have said something to her?"

"Whatta you mean?"

"Did you say anything to anyone else dealing or buying or taking?"

"Well, no, but—"

A skinny older couple stumbles out of the old, heavy wooden entry door to the bar, holding on to one another as if on ice skates.

We watch them for a few moments. Dawson takes a step toward them and starts to say something when it looks like they're heading for one of the vehicles in the side lot, but stops as an Uber pulls up and they begin to negotiate their way into the backseat.

"Did you have an inappropriate relationship with Blake?"

"*No. Never.* I wouldn't—I was just lookin' out for her."

"Why?"

"Because," he says, "she wasn't like the rest of them. She was . . . There was something very special about her. She was an incredible young woman, the kind I could see being my little sister. I just tried to make sure she was okay. That's it. That's all. Don't try to take something good I did and twist it into something sick."

"So Blake had nothing to do with and wasn't around any—"

"Everyone in the bar was *around* it," he says. "It was happening all over the place, but no . . . she . . . ."

I can tell something is occurring to him as he talks.

"What is it?" I say.

"She asked me to give her a tour of the barge," he says. "Like I said, she was smarter, more curious than all the rest of 'em combined. I was showin' her around when Mr. Richards came up and said I was needed for a fight on deck and he'd finish the tour. I've never thought anything of it . . . but . . . what if she saw or heard something she wasn't supposed to—or he thought she did. Oh my God, I can't believe I didn't see it before. If he had something to do with it, I'll . . . ."

36

"Anna and I want you to know how much we love you and how proud we are of you," I'm saying to Nash. "We appreciate how well you're doing in school, how you are with Taylor and Johanna, how you treat Natalie, and the work you put in the guitar."

"Thank you, John," he says.

It hasn't come up and I'm not sure if or when it will, but I'm hoping at some point he will call me Dad—and he'll do so because I really feel like and function as his father.

"It's been an unimaginably difficult year for you," Anna says, "and you've responded to all the tragedies and challenges like few people could."

He nods but doesn't speak. His eyes are moist and his lip quivers a little.

Before he gets completely overwhelmed, I say, "We got you something. If you don't like it or want a different type or color or want something else entirely, we can take it back, so be honest, okay?"

He nods vigorously. "Okay, but I'm sure I'll love it. And thank y'all so much."

"Taylor, can you help me get it?"

She jumps up from the couch and we rush into the mud room where the guitar box is hidden beneath a blanket.

As we bring it through the kitchen toward where he's waiting in the living room, Taylor says, "Okay, close your eyes and hold out your hands."

By the time we reach the living room, Nash is standing up and has complied.

"Hold 'em out more," Taylor says. "It's *big*."

He extends his arms even more and we ease the rectangular cardboard box onto them.

"Okay," Taylor says, "open your eyes."

I think it's a good sign that she is so happy Nash is getting a gift.

When he opens his eyes he says, "You got me a small surfboard? Cool."

"Open it. Open it," Taylor says.

He backs up and sits down on the couch, and opens the box now balanced on his knees.

When he sees the Squier Paranormal Toronado he lets out an audible gasp and the moistness in his eyes trickles out.

"Oh my God," he says. "I love it. It's so . . . *cool*. Wow, it's beautiful."

"For when you're ready to rock," I say.

"I'm ready," he says.

He removes the guitar from the box and lets the box slide down his extended legs to the floor.

"I love the color," he says.

"It's Lake Placid-blue," I say.

"If you don't like it—"Anna says.

"*Like it*? I *love* it."

"But if there's something else you'd rather have—"

"Just try to get it away from me," he says.

"John saw it when he went into Leitz to get your strings and just grabbed it for you," she says, "but we can take you back and you can pick out the one—"

"*This* is the one," he says. "It's perfect. I couldn't . . . love it any more. Thank you guys so, so much."

As he tunes it and begins to strum it, I realize the mistake I've made.

"Looks like we'll be going back to the music store anyway," I say. "It never even crossed my mind to get an amp."

"That's okay," he says. "I don't need—"

"No, it's not. It's a rookie mistake. But we'll fix it. And for tonight we can borrow an amp from a buddy of mine so you can—"

"You don't have to—"

"Yes, I do," I say. "I want you to be able to play it tonight. I'll give him a call and go grab it now. You just be ready to rock when I get back."

"*Rock and roll*," Taylor shouts, holding up hand-horns. "*Rock and roll*."

37

N ash is playing "Rock and Roll All Nite" by Kiss as he and Taylor dance and sing. Anna and I are sitting next to each other on the couch enjoying the show.

Taylor is on the coffee table and is nearly as tall as Nash is, and they're both bringing intense rock star energy.

As always in situations like this, I have a pang of guilt and sadness that Johanna can't be here with us.

"He's really good," I say to Anna.

She nods. "This was a great thing you did, John Jordan."

"I'm gonna FaceTime Johanna so she can hear him."

"That's a great idea," she says.

I call Johanna and hold the phone up for her to hear the end of the song. As soon as the song is completed, I say, "Check out Nash's new ax."

"Wow. Very cool, dude," she says to him. "It's beautiful."

"It's Lake Placid-blue," he says.

"Play another one," she says. "Do you take requests?"

"Only if it's one of the handful of songs I already know," he says.

I wonder what it would've been like if Blake had been my

daughter and I had known it, what it would be like to have her here now—in person or by phone—participating in this.

I stand the phone against a small stack of books so Johanna has a front row seat, and sit back beside Anna and take her hand.

Before the next song starts, the three siblings discuss various topics, including the girls learning instruments and the three of them starting a band.

"So," Anna whispers, "Trevor King claims he didn't get Blake's *come and get me* text, but . . . it was opened and read within minutes of her sending it. And it was early enough in the evening that he was still up. Maybe his phone wasn't with him and someone else looked at the text, but I doubt it, and if they had, wouldn't they have shown it to him right away?"

"You would think," I say. "Unless it was someone with a motive not to—someone wanting him to stay at the party and for Blake not to attend."

"Like an ex?" she says. "'Cause Trevor had one there—according to his deposition. She's one of the people who give him an alibi."

"Interesting," I say.

"*I* thought so," she says.

"What's her name?"

"Missy," she says. "Missy Arnold."

"What about his phone?" I ask. "Did it ping off any towers—"

"Looks like it never left his apartment," she says.

"Figured that was the case," I say, "but wanted to make sure."

"I suspect him more now than I did before," she says. "I don't think there's any way he didn't see her text. I think it's possible he left his phone there so as not to be tracked."

"Which would show premeditation," I say. "That's a whole other level of—"

"There's no way we can get them," she says, "but I'd be interested to see Missy's phone records. See if her phone pinged off any towers up here that night."

I start to say something, but Nash begins playing "Whole Lotta Love" by Led Zeppelin.

38

"John," Sandy is saying, "this poor girl was murdered. I'm as certain of that as I can be, given what I have to work with."

With my family long since in bed asleep, I'm on a laptop at the kitchen table on a Zoom meeting with Sandy Lewis, who's been looking over the autopsy photos I forwarded to her. I value and trust her forensic opinions as much as anyone's on the planet.

Sandy is on a laptop of her own in bed, her partner Christy propped up on pillows reading a novel beside her.

"She never says things that definitively," Christy says.

"I'm convinced," Sandy says.

"Then so am I," I say, though I already was.

"Plus, I'm unofficial now," Sandy says. "I can afford to be more forceful with my opinions. And I'm absolutely appalled at the job the medical examiner did in this case."

"*Absolutely appalled*," Christy says. "Better look out now."

"I'm not sayin' she didn't have a fall," Sandy says to me, ignoring Christy, "but even if she did, she was assaulted first. And possibly raped. The injures to her nose and lip don't have the accompanying abrasions I'd expect to see if she hit her face on a rock, or a tree, or even the ground. Her hands and arms have what appear to be defensive wounds. And if she fell from a great height and hit an object hard enough and with enough force to make the wounds she sustained, I'd expect her to have broken bones. She has none. The ME concludes that she died as the result of blunt force trauma to her head, but if she fell eighty, ninety, a hundred feet and hit her head on a rock or a log or a boat, I'd expect to see far, far more significant damage to her skull. The injuries she has are far more consistent with her being assaulted and being struck on the head with a hard object swung with force or having her head slammed into it, not falling from a great height and striking it."

I feel the pain of each injury as she describes them, as if I have an even deeper connection with Blake than most of the other victims I become a surrogate for. Am I imagining it or are we linked, joined, related?

"What about rape?" I ask.

"The bruising to her inner thighs is the type we often see in sexual assault," she says. "And the injuries to her neck and throat are consistent with being choked and forcible oral sex. But we'll never know for sure because a rape kit wasn't performed. It's . . . not just perplexing . . . it's . . . it's negligence is what it is."

I feel like I'm going to throw up, and swallow hard against it. My skin is clammy and sweat is popping out on my brow. I take a deep breath and let it out slowly, trying not to let on to Sandy the condition I'm in.

"*Negligence*," Christy says. "You've unleashed the beast now, John. Is there anything she won't say?"

Sandy's focus on her findings and interaction with Christy causes her not to notice how what she's saying is affecting me.

"I won't say any of this officially," she says. "It's why I'm talking like this. None of this is going to help you build a case, but ... it may aid you in finding the truth."

"That's the best I can hope for at this point," I say. "What else?"

"I'm not sure if the mark on her abdomen is from a bite," she says. "The pictures are of too low a quality to tell, but I believe it is."

"That's good enough for me," I say.

"She was found floating facedown, correct?"

I nod.

"The fixed lividity of the body reveals that she was face down after death. Doesn't tell us for sure she was in the water that entire time, but it doesn't contradict it. However, the triangular mark on her chest suggests that her body rested on an object that shape post-mortem, so unless there was something in the water beneath her ... and even then it would have to stay with her while the current carried her along, and it's hard to imagine with the buoyancy of her body in the water that it could press against something that hard for that long to make it ... I'd say following her death she rested on something that created that mark and then later was moved into the water. Now, it's possible she fell from somewhere lower on the bluff and landed on something on the side that created the mark, but then the question becomes how did her body get into the water? And I still believe she was assaulted antemortem. So I have a theory for you."

"Let's hear it."

"Hell has frozen over and the world is coming to an end," Christy says. "She's actually positing a theory."

"As a plain old public citizen," she says. "And completely unofficially, I certainly am. If someone attacked and killed her —as part of a sexual assault or in some other scenario, then dragged her body down the bluff and placed it face down over the front bow of the canoe . . . You did say they were using a canoe, correct?"

"Yes," I say. "They were."

"I think it's possible the bow of the canoe could've made that mark if her body was draped over it."

"That's genius," I say.

"We'd have to know what kind of canoe they had and do some controlled experiments to be sure, but . . . I believe it *is* possible."

39

T he next morning I meet with Jasper Wallace, the Potter County sheriff's investigator who mishandled Blake's case.

We are meeting with Dad in his office, which is the only way Jasper would agree to talk to me.

Dad and I haven't spoken since he refused to give me the file and told me not to take this case, and the only communication we've had was his blistering voicemail.

The atmosphere around us is tense and awkward, his anger and annoyance with me palpable.

"Before we begin," Dad says, "get Merrill in here too."

Jasper nods, gets up, goes to the door, opens it, and yells for Merrill.

When Merrill reaches the doorframe, which he nearly fills, he stands there, raising his head and eyebrows to Dad.

"Will you join us for this?" Dad says. "Since you've been helpin' John in the investigation anyway . . . think you should hear this."

Merrill closes the door and takes the only other empty seat in the room.

Jasper says, "Let me start by sayin' I don't appreciate y'all goin' behind me and reinvestigating my case. The fact that all the others who've looked at this case, including that black PI, should let y'all know there's nothing there, but y'all got to be . . ." He glances at Dad, seems to think better about what he was about to say, then he looks back at me. "Well, it just shows a lot of arrogance to think you can do my job better than me. And you," he adds, turning to Merrill, "you sneaking 'round here in your own department stealin' information . . . that's a betrayal like none of us has ever seen before. You don't do that. I know he's your friend, but . . . it's like being on a team and playing against another team. You can have friends on that other team, and when you come off the field you can be friends again, but you don't betray your teammates. You never betray your teammates."

"The only betrayal done in this case is to your badge," I say. "You didn't do an adequate investigation and you and everyone else know it."

"Oh, I betrayed my badge? Really? You arrogant asshole. How dare you say that shit to me."

"I'm here today to ask why," I say. "Why did you not really investigate this case? From what I've been able to tell, you usually don't do this bad of a job, so why did you on this one?"

"I don't think I done a bad job on it," he says. "It was an accident. The poor girl drank too much and fell off the cliff. It's sad and tragic, and they should've never been up on that bluff in the first place, but it *was* an accident."

"It may have been," I say, "but without a thorough investigation we can't know for sure."

"That's the thing," he says. "No matter what I did or didn't do, no matter what you and the black PI and everyone else does, it won't change the fact that it was an accident. No one killed that girl."

"Why didn't you order a rape kit?" I ask.

"No cop I know would order a rape kit on an accidental drowning."

"She didn't die from drowning," I say.

"You know what I meant. Plus she was on her period. She had a tampon in."

"You say no cop you know would've ordered a rape kit," I say, "but no experienced investigator I know would say you did an adequate investigation—or that you did much of an investigation at all."

He shrugs. "So?"

I'm looking at Jasper, not Dad, but I can hear him shift in his chair and sigh.

"Why didn't you listen to Dawson Lightner and Thad Jones?" I say. "They were telling you there was enough suspicion to warrant a real investigation."

"No off-duty deputy and some quota cop gonna tell me how to do my damn job."

"Quota cop?" Merrill says.

"Take offense if you want to, snowflake, but he only has that job 'cause they didn't base the hire on merit or experience."

"Let's stay on topic," Dad says.

Merrill nods then looks at Jasper. "Whatcha say you and I have this discussion another time?"

"Anytime, anywhere."

"Why didn't you process the crime scene and preserve evidence?" I ask.

"There was *no* crime scene," he says. "There was *no* evidence."

"Sure there was," I say, "but even if there wasn't, you couldn't know for sure unless you did an investigation. Had you been drinking?"

"What?"

"Before you showed up to the scene that day," I say. "Several witnesses say they smelled it on you."

"It was a holiday weekend," he says. "I wasn't even supposed be on call, but the sheriff was out of town and the investigator who was supposed to be working was in the hospital with a burst appendix. I'd had a few, but I'll tell you this . . . I could've had a few suitcases of beer and it wouldn't've changed anything. It was an accident."

"So your method is take a quick look and determine whether it's homicide, suicide, or accident and go with that?"

"Oh, it's so easy to Monday morning quarterback, but I was there. Not you. Not any of you. I know what it was."

"Bein' there got nothin' to do with it," Merrill says. "Sometimes that herd you hear approaching isn't horses but zebras."

"What?" Jasper says. "What the hell does that mean?"

"What happened to Blake's things?" I ask. "They were never returned to her mother."

Dad looks at Jasper. Jasper shrugs.

"Were they logged into evidence?" Dad asks.

"Evidence of what?" Jasper says. "Her friends said they would take her things to her mom."

"Let's talk about those supposed friends," I say. "Two of the three had criminal records and all of them were acting suspicious, and yet they were never treated like suspects, never even properly questioned. And their statements read like they were written by small children."

Jasper looks at Dad and Dad frowns and nods.

"What he's about to tell you can't leave this room," Dad says. "No matter what. Not a word. Not even to the mom. Y'all haven't earned the trust we're about to give you on this case, but don't make me regret this."

"I interviewed them," Jasper says. "Even though it was obvious it was an accident. And I was going to again, do a follow up after the autopsy and everything, but . . . I got a call from a Bridgeport detective. Said they were confidential informants and he'd appreciate if we'd cut 'em loose, keep 'em out of it. And since it was an accident anyway . . ."

"He said all three of them were CIs?" I say.

"Maybe not. I can't remember. But he asked us to leave them out of it. And like I say, I was gonna leave them out anyway since it was an accident."

"Bottom line is this," Dad says. "Could Jasper have done more? Yes. Should he have? Sure. Would it have changed the outcome? Absolutely not. And there's a certain kind of cruelty in exploiting the mother's need to blame someone rather than forcing her to face the facts."

40

"W e were after Elon DeVaughn and Don Richards," Will Crews says. "Among others. Brody and Kieran were smalltime, but they're who we had, so to save their asses from jail time, they became CIs."

Will Crews, a detective with Bridgeport PD, is a friend of Kathryn's and didn't hesitate when she asked if he'd be willing to answer a few questions for me about Brody and Kieran.

He called me within minutes of me hanging up with her.

I talk to him as I drive toward St. Ann's.

"It was a whole task force with FDLE, Fish and Game, and ATF," he says. "I was one small cog, but I was the one who had arrested Brody and Kieran for the thirteenth time and had turned them into CIs, so that was my ticket in. But I didn't have much to do with any of it. Nothing operational or anything . . . just attended a few meetings, was CCed on a few emails, and talked to Brody and Kieran a few times."

"Tell me about them," I say. "What'd all you arrest them for?"

"They're spoiled, entitled, alcoholic, drug-addicted assholes," he says. "Most of what they were arrested for is related to that, but nearly all of it had a violent component. They deal some, but just enough to support their own habits and be able to play instead of work. We've gotten them on DUIs, leaving the scene of an accident, assault, grand theft, possession, intent, battery. Can't tell you how many girls Brody beat the shit out of who went right back to him. They're not violent when they're sober—if you can ever catch them that way—but as soon as they're on the shit, they get vicious, especially Brody. And you know the damnedest thing about it all, the only reason most of the girls aren't with Brody's sadistic ass right now is because he won't have them, not the other way around. I just . . . can't even wrap my head around that."

I nod though he can't see me, and think about the dynamic between the abused and their abusers.

"I wish I had known Blake was anywhere near them that weekend," he says. "I'd've gone up there and gotten her myself —arrested her if I had to. I just didn't know."

I drive through a light rain shower so brief my wipers only make three passes across the windshield, and when I reach Highway 98, the sun is so bright over the Gulf it makes it difficult to see.

"Feeling about Kathryn and Blake the way you do, and knowing Brody and Kieran's history," I say, "it surprises me that you told Jasper to back off them."

"Never said anything of the dang kind," he says. "I let him know they were CIs and offered to help him if he needed leverage with them. Told him if they were involved in Blake's death our deal with them was off. He told me her death was an accident. I told him to be sure. To let us know and we could get their help on Richards and DeVaughn right before we arrested them for Blake's death. Never heard from him again."

"That's not the story he's telling now," I say.

"Then he's lying."

"What happened with the investigation into Richards and DeVaughn?" I ask.

"I assume it's still ongoing, but don't know for sure. Somebody way above my pay grade dropped Brody and Kieran, and as I was only involved because they were my CIs, I was out."

"No idea why they moved off of them?"

"My guess is they could tell they weren't going to get anything from them," he says. "DeVaughn and Richards are both too experienced to let two young punks like Brody and Kieran bring them down."

41

I find Kathryn in the mounted porch swing down by the lake at St. Ann's, most of the way through a bottle of chardonnay. She has two glasses as if expecting me, though I hadn't told her I was stopping by.

I tell her what Will Crews said as she refills her glass and pours the remaining two fingers into mine.

"Who the hell was my little girl up on that cliff with?" Kathryn says.

She's not slurring her words, but the effects of the wine on her are undeniable. Far more demonstrative than she usually is, she's also more animated and touchy.

"Some bad guys with connections to some worse guys," I say.

"Is it possible she saw something she wasn't supposed to and they killed her to cover it up—either Brody and Kieran or Elon DeVaughn or Don Richards?"

"It's possible," I say. "Dawson said Richards gave Blake a tour of the barge, so . . ."

"Maybe Bri really doesn't have anything to do with it," she says.

"I'm not ready to rule her out," I say. "And even if she wasn't directly involved in the murder, she was probably involved in the cover-up. There's got to be a reason they got married and moved so soon afterwards—especially since they hadn't been dating long."

"Yeah, that's true, but . . . I feel like Bri just always needs a man. She would've probably said yes to any proposal. Could be Brody covering his ass instead of them being partners in it."

"Certainly a possibility."

"Will we ever get to the truth?" she says. "I'm beginning to lose faith that we will."

"Told you I wouldn't stop until I do," I say.

"Everywhere I look around here I see her," she says. "I watched her grow up here. Every birthday, every holiday, every-thing. Learning to ride her bike. Playing with her friends. Hunting Easter eggs. Trying out new Christmas toys. Building forts and decorating for Halloween. There's not a single place I can look that I don't have a memory for."

"I'm so, so sorry."

"I should've told you," she said. "Should've told her about you."

She should've found out who her father was and told him —whether it was me or Steve—and told Blake, but I'm assuming that's what she means.

"I just keep thinking how different our lives would've been if I had. I can't help but believe she'd still be alive today if I had."

I don't say anything, just listen.

"You and I would've been good together," she says.

I won't let myself go there.

"You know?" she says, turning toward me. "And you would've protected our little girl. Wouldn't you? You would have. I know it."

Suddenly, before I realize what she's doing, she leans in and kisses me.

It's a hard, passionate kiss that has the sweet, fruity smell of chardonnay.

Without returning the kiss and without snatching away, I slowly pull back.

She opens her eyes and looks at me, her face still close to mine. "I'm *so* sorry," she whispers. "I . . . I'm not sure what to say. I did it before I realized what I was doing."

"I understand," I say.

"Please don't quit the case because I . . . behaved badly."

"I'm not going to quit."

"I can't believe I just lunged at you like that. I'm so embarrassed."

"Don't be," I say. "Please don't give it another thought."

"I'm so pathetic," she says. "Such a . . . No wonder God took my little girl."

"None of that's true," I say. "You're just—"

"Please don't tell Anna," she says.

"It's no big deal," I say. "Don't worry about it, but I have to. I can't keep—"

"Oh God," she says. "She'll make you quit and probably kick my ass."

"It's okay and it's no big deal, but I can't keep something like that from her. I promise she won't do anything."

"She won't have to do anything," she says. "I'm gonna die of embarrassment first."

42

"I told you, didn't I?" Anna says.

"You did."

Actually, she just said she didn't want me working for Kathryn. I don't recall her telling me she'd have a bottle of wine and try to kiss me.

Though driving home to her, I call Anna as soon as I leave St. Ann's and let her know what happened. If I could've called her and told her *while* it was happening I would have.

"You should always trust me on these things."

"I do."

"You always believe the best in people, but I told you."

"She'd just had too much to drink and was feeling—"

"Horny?"

"I was gonna say *vulnerable*."

"You never think women are into you," she says. "Even when it's obvious they are. Did you kiss her back?"

"Not in the slightest."

"I believe you," she says. "And I can't tell you how good that makes me feel."

"She said to apologize to you," I say. "She's very embarrassed."

"You told her you were going to tell me?" she asks.

"Of course."

"Thank you," she says.

"Of course."

"She's embarrassed . . ." she says. "But . . . bet she wouldn't be if you had responded differently."

"Well, we'll never know."

"No we won't," she says, "but I'll tell you what I *do* know. I know somebody who's gettin' some passionate kisses when he gets home—*if* he washes his lips first."

LATER THAT NIGHT, Merrill and I, with the help of off-duty cops and friends, begin unofficial surveillance of Don Richards's Barge Bar.

We take the first shift, maneuvering Jake's boat into a slough upriver, and using night vision binoculars to watch the barge and the area around it.

"Think my days in your dad's department are numbered," he says. "One way or another."

"Because of what I asked you to do?"

"You didn't ask me. I offered."

"What has he said?" I ask.

He shrugs, which I sense more than see in the darkness. "Not a lot. Said how disappointed he was, how trust had been violated, and at a minimum there'd be a reprimand, but that we'd talk about it soon."

"Sorry," I say. "But a reprimand isn't a termination."

"Nah, but that was the minimum, so I figure there's still a chance he lets me go. Or . . . a chance he loses the election. Or . . . more likely . . . I turn in my two weeks. Only reason I've been stayin' is tryin' to change the culture. You have any idea how many white supremacist sympathizers there are in that one little department?"

"If there's even one it's way too many," I say.

"I wish it were one," he says with a sigh and a harsh, humorless laugh. "I don't mean they attend Klan rallies, but without most of them even realizing it they defer to white people and harass black people—and only a small part of that is related to socio-economic issues. It's no wonder black people get not just arrested but shot at such higher rates. I thought I could help change some hearts and minds, but . . . it'd take a generation—and only then with the sheriff's support. And that's somethin' I ain't got right now."

I let out a long, heavy sigh. "I don't know that I've ever been as discouraged by humanity as I am right now."

"'Bout time you came around," he says.

"The levels of selfishness," I say. "The celebration of ignorance. The disrespect and disregard for others who disagree. The tribalism. The lack of empathy and listening. I—"

Don Richards appears at the top of the barge, climbs down the ladder, boards his boat, and pulls away.

"Want to follow him?" Merrill asks.

"Nah," I say. "But we can probably call it a night."

"Don't know," Merrill says. "Be smart of him not to be onboard when product arrives or is distributed."

EVEN LATER THAT night I wake up screaming from a nightmare in which I had a daughter who resembled Blake that I couldn't protect. Everywhere she turned, evil men wanted to rape and kill her, evil women wanted to eliminate her as a threat, and there was nothing I could do about it. By the end of the ordeal —or at least the point at which I scream myself awake—an insidious incubus resembling Brody was simultaneously raping and murdering my little girl while a figure resembling Bri was telling him what to do to her as Elon DeVaughn, Kieran McClellan, and the others from River Fest restrained me and forced me to watch.

43

The next morning with very little sleep, I pay a surprise visit to Bri Allen after Brody leaves for work.

She is small, both short and thin, and has the appearance of a teenager. She's not unattractive. She's just not particularly pretty. Not plain exactly, but all her features, while not unpleasing, seem to blend together, lacking any distinctness that would distinguish them in any way. She talks fast and says a lot even when she's not saying much, and she has the nervousness of a stray cat living on a mean street.

We are seated at a glass dining room table in their condo on the west end of Panama City Beach. Beyond the bay window behind her, the Gulf of Mexico is calm beneath a bright morning sun, the gently undulating waters seeming an even deeper shade of green—more jade than its usual emerald.

"I feel bad for . . ." she says. "For Blake—and for her mom. Always have. But . . . the shit she has put us through. It's been hell on us too. And nobody cares because they think we're guilty, but . . . what if we're innocent? Is it still okay that we've been treated the way we have?"

I've explained to her who I am and what I'm doing and why.

I've let her know that I'm working for Kathryn and that I only want to find the truth—and I'm open to whatever that is.

"I have . . . The thing is . . . I feel like I have nothing to hide, but . . . there are certain . . . parties . . . who think I shouldn't talk to anyone without a lawyer."

"I understand," I say. "I promise I'm not here to try to trick you or trip you up. I just want to hear your side of things directly from you and ask you a few questions."

"I don't know . . ."

"What about this?" I say. "We each record our conversation with our phones, that way you'll have a record of exactly what we said. If I ever try to say or imply anything false or misleading, you'll have the proof of what you actually said. And, of course, you can stop the interview anytime you like."

"Well, I guess . . . that would be . . . okay. You seem like a very nice man."

"I am," I say.

The high-rise beach-side condo is far pricier than they should be able to afford, but the furniture looks to have come with it and been used and abused by hundreds of renters. And though they are living here, there's very little here that's actually theirs. It's as if I could be here visiting someone on vacation.

"Just start by telling me what happened."

"I don't know what happened," she says. "That's the thing. I have no idea what happened to Blake. We were trashed. I passed out the moment my head hit the pillow and I didn't move until the next morning."

"Where did you sleep?"

"In the tent," she says. "Brody and I had it the first night and Kieran and Blake were supposed to have it the second, but . . . Kieran was too fucked-up to even get back up there when we got back so we left him sleeping in the boat. No way we could carry him. And when the three of us got to the top, Brody started saying the three of us should sleep in it, like, you know, Blake could join us since it was just us, but I said *no*. No way. The deal was we got it the first night and they got it the second night, but Brody kicks off his flip-flops and goes in the tent and collapses on the air mattress anyway. Blake said it was okay. That I should join him and that she didn't mind being in the hammock again. Said she was so tired she could sleep anywhere. She was a really nice girl. She had her . . . stuff like everybody else, but she was a good person and a good friend."

"So you and Brody were in the tent, Blake was in one of the hammocks, and Kieran was in the boat at the base of the cliff?"

She nods. "That's the way we started. I swear it on my mother's life."

"But that's not how it was the next morning, was it?" I ask.

"No. When I came out of the tent—and I was the first one out, Brody was still asleep—Kieran was up there with us. He was asleep in a hammock and Blake was gone."

That lines up with what Kieran said, but is it a story they've come up with to try to control the narrative or is it what actually happened? And if it's a story, why would Kieran go along with it since it makes him look the most suspicious?

"I don't think for one minute Kieran hurt her or did anything but wake up in the boat, climb up, and crawl into a hammock. He said she wasn't out there when he did, so whatever happened to her must have happened before he came up. He said he just thought she was in the tent with us. I believe him. He's a mess—drinks too much and acts like a junior high boy—but he's not violent. He's not a killer."

"So you went to sleep as soon as you got up there and didn't wake up or get up until the next morning?"

"Yeah," she says. "Well, I guess . . . I woke up one time and Brody was fuckin' me. But I fell back asleep and didn't wake up or get up again."

"Not even to pee?"

She shakes her head. "I had to go so bad the next morning I was surprised I hadn't wet myself."

"And Blake was gone?"

She nods, makes a sad expression, and seems about to cry.

"But her things were there?" I ask.

"Yeah, most of them. Her clothes, shoes, phone, keys. That kind of stuff. She . . . It wasn't everything she had. I didn't think she was naked wherever she was, but it was most of her things."

"I thought y'all had hidden her keys so she wouldn't drive home drunk?"

"We did. One of the guys must have returned them."

"A lot has been made about what Blake was wearing," I say. "Her mom says she didn't have any bright pink shorts like the ones she was found in."

"Blake wasn't sure she'd stay Saturday night," she says. "Anyway, she didn't bring enough clothes. And ol' Creepy Cop knocked her drink into her, so the clothes she did have smelled like booze and were sticky with fruit juice. I let her borrow some of mine. She was undressing out there as I was about to go into the tent and I took off my shorts and threw them to her. Didn't need them anyway at that point. I told her to grab one of my shirts from the line, that it should be dry by now. The bathing suit she had on underneath was fine. She just needed shorts and a shirt. See? It's that simple. All these crazy theories and suspicions over nothing."

"With all or most of her things there," I say, "why would you think she might have gone back to the bar or to the houseboat Cameron Perry was on?"

"I didn't," she says. "I thought she was . . . I thought maybe she had gone to pee or was still up there on the bluff some-where, but . . . when we didn't find her . . . I started getting worried."

"So why did you say she could've gone back to the bar or gotten on a houseboat or went to see her ex?" I ask again.

"I didn't want her to be dead," she says. "I was just hoping it was something else. I wasn't—I know people have said I changed my story, but I wasn't . . . I was just upset and confused and saying what I hoped might have happened, but I knew. I knew the moment they found the body over there that it was her."

"How?"

"I just did."

"Did you see something or hear something that made you think that?"

She shakes her head. "No. I just knew."

"Did something happen or someone say something that maybe didn't mean anything at the time, but when she went missing or when the body was found made you think something bad had happened?"

"No. Nothing like that. I just knew. It's like . . . we had a connection and I felt when she wasn't, like, connected to me anymore, 'cause she was gone."

"Why didn't y'all report her missing or look for her?"

"We did," she says. "That's another thing that makes me so mad. Everyone acts like all we did was ignore the fact that our friend was missing and then played on the river all day. No. We told people and we asked around for her and we looked. I mean a lot. Did we also do a few River Fest things too? Yeah. Do I wish we hadn't? I guess. But Blake was already dead. Nothin' we could've done for her."

"But you didn't know that at the time, right?"

"Right."

"Or did you? Did you—"

"You said you weren't going to try to trick me or . . . bully me."

"I'm not," I say. "I'm not trying to do either. I promise you."

"I didn't know she was already dead . . . I'm just sayin' once I knew . . . I don't know . . . I guess that she would've understood and would've wanted us to . . . have a nice time. I think she would've done the same if I went missing."

I think about the pictures the three of them took on that Sunday—how happy, how much fun they were having. There's not a single image that shows the slightest sign of worry or concern. I also think about Kieran posting that it was the *best weekend ever*.

"Who is Creepy Cop?" I ask, as if I don't know who she was referring to. "And how did he spill Blake's drink on her?"

"That's what we called the security guy," she says. "Dawson Creek Creepy Cop. He's an off-duty cop. He's overly friendly with some of the girls—but nobody more than Blake. He was doing his usual flirting shit and he got too aggressive and knocked her drink all over her. Acted like he was on something. He was worse than usual."

"Did he do anything else?"

"Every time you turned around he was near her or watching her."

"Did he ever visit the campsite?"

She shakes her head. "Not that I know. And I'm not accusing him of anything. I know what it's like to be accused without any . . . you know, evidence or anything . . . and no one believing you no matter what you say or do."

"Yeah," I say, "it's unfair and I know it can be hurtful."

"The things people say online," she says. "Trolls or whatever they call them. *They . . . are . . . so . . . mean.*"

Everything she says makes her sound young, naive, innocent, but nothing so much as calling internet trolls *mean*. It's hard to juxtapose this with the image of her going crazy and beating up Claire.

"I'm hoping my investigation will help with that," I say. "And that's certainly what Blake's mom wants. She wants the truth of what happened to her daughter to come out and she doesn't want anyone falsely accused of anything."

"See, I feel like *she's* falsely accused *me*," she says.

"Really?"

"Well, yeah. She keeps saying Blake was killed, that she didn't die of an accidental fall, and that we're responsible. That we . . . killed her or . . . I don't know, covered it up or something."

"I think she's been frustrated with the lack of cooperation and information coming out," I say. "From what I've seen she's asking questions more than making accusations, but I know she was especially disappointed y'all plead the Fifth."

"I was disappointed she sued us for millions of dollars we don't have, but . . . the Fifth thing was what Brody's lawyers told us to do. I want to talk. I'm talking to you."

"Yes you are and I appreciate it. Let's go back to Creepy Cop and the Barge Bar. Did he do anything else or did anyone else?"

She shrugs and twists her lips as she seems to think about it. "I don't guess so."

"I know there was a lot of drinking going on," I say.

"Yeah."

"And some drug use."

"Yeah, I guess. That's not my—I don't do drugs, so . . . I don't know much about that, but it was definitely around."

"I heard there were some altercations in the bar that night," I say.

She shrugs again. "I guess."

"Several people had exes there and—"

"Oh, yeah. One of the things River Fest is, is showing off your new boo to your ex or exes. People get jealous. People drink and get flirty and . . . I don't know . . . riled up. But it's usually no big deal. I got upset with one of Brody's exes and even hit her, but I apologized the next day when I was sober and it was all cool. We even bought each other a drink. I think most of it's like that. Especially with the girls. The guys usually don't make up or anything but they don't keep trying to fight—until they get drunk again."

"What all did Brody do to make you jealous?"

She shakes her head. "He's just a big flirt. 'Specially when he's drinkin'."

"Did he flirt with Blake?"

"He flirted with everybody," she says. "Even Kieran. He's just that way. Don't mean anything by it. But some people take it the wrong way."

"What about Cameron Perry?" I ask.

"What about him?"

"You said you thought Blake might have left to go hook up with him."

"Wasn't tryin' to accuse him of anything. He just— Blake wasn't done with him. I don't think she wanted to drop Trevor and get back with Cam, but . . . she didn't like seein' him with Hailey. Made her crazy he was moving on. She said she'd like to do him that weekend . . . just to remind him how good she was, keep him on the string."

"She told you that?"

"Not in so many words, but yeah. Plus I knew her. I knew how she was. How she thinks."

I wonder how well she really knew Blake and how much she's projecting onto her.

"Were Kieran and Brody doing drugs?" I ask.

"I . . . I'd rather not . . . I don't know for sure. Like I said, not my thing. And I don't want to . . . I just want to talk about what I know for sure and about what I saw and what I did. Let others speak for themselves."

I nod. "I understand. And that's wise. Since it happened, since you've had all this time to look back on it, has anything come to mind that may explain exactly what happened? Has anyone said or done anything that makes you think different about anything?"

She shrugs. "Not really. I stopped going on social media, so . . . I don't hear much of anything about—"

A door opens down the hallway and a thin thirty-something white man in swim trunks and no shirt with dark hair and pale skin stumbles out.

I'm pretty sure it's Elon DeVaughn. The pictures I've seen of him are nearly five years old and he's changed a lot, but I'm pretty sure it's him.

Rookie mistake. I hadn't known anyone else was here.

Bri's body language changes. She tenses up and suddenly becomes both more rigid and fidgety.

"The fuck are you?" he says to me. "The fuck is he?" he says, turning toward Bri.

"This is John. We've just been talkin' about—"

"I heard what you've been talkin' about," he says. "And I called Brody. He's on his way back."

"You better go," she says to me.

"Are you okay?" I say to her.

"Yeah, I'm fine. He'll be mad, but he won't hit me or anything."

"Are you sure? Do you want to come with me? Do you want me to stay and talk to—"

"No, just go. It'll be okay."

"Why'd you let him in and talk to him in the first place?" he says.

"'Cause we haven't done anything wrong and have nothing to hide," she says. "I'm so ready for this to be over. I just want them to prove it was an accident and for everyone to leave us alone."

I stand up.

"You Elon?" I say.

"I'm your worst fuckin' nightmare if you don't get the fuck out of here," he says.

I laugh out loud. "You're a skinny, soft, underdeveloped

drug dealer who lives the hashtag yacht life. You're a *parent's* worst nightmare, but that's about it."

"Don't have to be big or strong to do damage," he says.

I shrug and give him an expression that says I'm not worried, though I'm dubious he might be right. "Well, do your best," I say.

"Didn't mean now," he says. "Hell, you're a cop with a gun in our home. No, I meant when you least expect it."

"I always expect little back shooters like you," I say. "You come at me and I'll put you down hard. But if by some miracle you heave a Hail Mary that gets through, I've got five friends I can think of off the top of my head that will hunt you down and square it within hours if not minutes of you doing anything, so . . . as I say . . . do your best."

The front door crashes open and slams into the wall behind it and Brody rushes in.

"You stupid fuckin' cunt," he says. "I told you—"

"He's different," she says. "And I'm tired of not talkin' about it. I want this to be over. I want to help Blake's mom find some peace."

"It'll never be over," he says. "Not ever. What about *our* peace? You want that bitch to have peace but she's the reason we don't. And he's not your friend. He's a fuckin' cop."

"Actually," I say, "I often get called Officer Friendly."

He spins around on me. "Get the fuck out of my house," he says. "Or—"

"Or what?" I say.

"I'll . . ."

"Always best to know what you're threatening before you start to make it," I say. "Also good idea to only make one you can back up."

"You have no right to be here," he says. "Leave now."

"Actually, Bri invited me in," I say.

"Well, her name ain't on the lease, so . . . I'm uninviting you."

"Brody, please," Bri says. "There's no need to be so—"

"I'll go," I say, "but before I do . . . I want you all to take a deep breath, settle down, and listen to me carefully."

I pause for a moment and look at each of them. I wait a little longer and a little of the tension seems to dissipate.

Unlike Elon, who has merely aged some, Brody doesn't just look older. He looks wrecked. His skin is pale and drawn, stretched over bone like a too-tight drumhead. His weary and wary eyes are unfocused and bloodshot—and have deep, dark half-circles beneath them. Five years further into adulthood and he's even thinner than he was before, and his unkempt hair is not just unstylishly shorter but already beginning to recede and thin.

Both Elon and Brody could have been involved in what happened to Blake, but whereas Brody shows the wear and tear of guilt and regret eating away at him, Elon shows no such effects. Maybe Brody is guilty and Elon is innocent, but I think it more likely that Elon is a self-centered sociopath incapable of feeling guilt or grief.

"I only want the truth," I say. "If you have nothing to hide, you have nothing to fear from me. If you are hiding something —a crime or a cover-up—it's in your best interest to come clean. Give yourself and Blake's mom some peace. Things get out of hand, especially when young people are drinking, so . . . everyone would understand."

I pause again but no one confesses to anything.

"What I'm about to say is the most important thing I'll say today, so listen carefully. Bri didn't say anything incriminating —about herself or anyone else. If anything, she went further in convincing me she's innocent. So I don't want to hear of either of you retaliating or bullying or intimidating her. And I and other cops will be checking back on her to make sure. I don't want to hear that either of you ever talk to her the way you have today. No more cussing her or calling her names or treating her like shit. Understand?"

Neither of them say anything.

"I want to hear that both of you understand," I say. "And that you understand this . . . If either of you lays a finger on her, I promise you I will pull your lives apart with a pair of pliers, piece by painful piece."

"You don't have to tell me how to treat my wife," Brody says. "I love her. I was upset before, but I didn't mean nothin' by what I said. And I'd never lay a hand on a woman."

"We have evidence of you doing just that," I say.

"I mean now," he says. "Claire don't count. We pushed each other's buttons and hurt each other. But I'm different now and Bri is a hell of a lot different than . . . anyone I've ever been with." He turns to her. "I'm sorry for how I talked to you, baby. I was just upset 'cause I work so hard to protect you and what we have, and maybe this guy isn't—I don't know—but plenty of people are trying to take away what we have."

I look from Brody to Elon.

He shakes his head. "That's as good as it's gonna get," he says. "Not gonna get any apologies from me. And you ain't gonna tell me how to or not to talk to some stupid little bitch who can't keep her mouth shut. And you ain't gonna do shit about what I do. I know my rights. I know no man gonna tell me what the fuck I can and can't do. Men a lot harder than you have tried and failed."

"If you do anything to her and I come after you," I say, "men a lot harder than me will come with me."

44

"So that's two people saying Kieran didn't go up when the rest of them did, but came up later," Kathryn is saying.

"And when he did," Addie says, "Blake was killed."

I meet Kathryn, Claire, and Addie at Blake's grave where, along with some big-boy help from Claire's son Corbin, they are cleaning it up and decorating it for fall.

This not only allows me to pay my respects to Blake, but to meet with Kathryn without being alone with her.

"I don't know," Claire says. "Sounds like it could've happened before he got up there."

"That's also another witness saying Dawson's attention was excessive," Kathryn says.

I turn to Addie and Claire. "Did either of you see him spill her drink on her?"

They nod.

"I bought that round," Claire says. "Carried all the drinks over without spilling a drop, then he bumps her hand and dumps hers all over her."

"Looked intentional to me," Addie says.

"You really think he meant to do it?" Kathryn says, then turning to Claire asks, "Do you?"

"He was awful quick to say he had extra clothes in his boat and to try to get her to go out there with him to put them on."

"I think that's why he did it," Addie says. "Trying to get her alone."

"Luckily she said no," Claire says. "She was polite but firm. Said it was fine, that she had her bathing suit underneath and didn't even feel it."

"Well, if you two didn't confirm it," Kathryn says, "I'd've thought Bri was just trying to put suspicion on other people."

"She probably is," Addie says. "It's just a spilt drink. And we don't know he did it on purpose or that he was trying to get her alone. No matter what he did or didn't do . . . Bri always throwin' shade."

"Yeah," Claire says, "she's still trying to make Cam look suspicious. Even Kieran to an extent. Anyone but her and Brody."

"And I can tell you buy her little innocent girl act," Addie says to me, "but—"

"I didn't buy anything," I say.

"But you found her convincing," Kathryn says.

"Didn't say I was convinced," I say. "Said it's possible she really doesn't know any more than she's said and that her contradictory statements may be—*may* be—the result of being upset and nervous and not very bright."

"Well, take it from me," Claire says, "it's all an act. And she perfected it over the years. She acts all innocent and naive and in need of being taken care of, but I've seen firsthand how vicious she can be."

"She said y'all made up."

"That was Brody's doing," Claire says. "After I went home Friday night I almost didn't come back on Saturday. I was just trying to avoid another scene and not have all of them mad at me. I went along with it because I was scared not to. They came up to me and Brody said, 'Bri's sorry. Please don't be mad at her. She doesn't have any girlfriends and is upset, thinks you hate her.' I went along with it to avoid anything else happening, but I'd never turn my back on any of them."

"I wish Blake wouldn't have," Addie says.

"I should have . . ." Claire says. "I tried to warn her, but . . . I should've been more . . . I should've made her come with me. I wish to God I had."

"We all do."

"What about DeVaughn?" Kathryn says. "What's his deal? Is he living with them?"

"He seemed pretty at home," I say. "And he's definitely helping Brody control Bri. But . . . he may be controlling both of them. He acts like he's untouchable."

"I hope you show him he's not," Addie says.

I smile. "Bet on it," I say. "Before this is over, our handprints will be all over his life."

45

"Elon DeVaughn is a pure sociopath."

I'm on the phone with Andy Spenser, an ATF agent on the task force with Will Crews from Bridgeport PD. Crews set up the call.

"He's very, very dangerous. And I don't just mean in your typical drug dealer way or even backed into a corner bad-guy way. It's not just that the guy has no conscience—he seems to enjoy inflicting pain on people. And he don't care what kind— mental, emotional, sexual, physical. All of the above."

I wonder which types he's inflicting on Bri.

"We can't make a case yet," he says, "and probably never will be able to, but I'm pretty sure he's killed at least three people. And it wasn't in deals gone down wrong or some kind of gangland shootout. It was far more . . . intimate. One on one. With a knife. And not just killing but carving."

He seems like the type. He's small and soft, but when I was around him I could feel evil emanating from him.

"Witnesses are scared of him—and with good reason," he adds. "They'd rather do time than testify against him. And the one or two that thought they'd rather flip on him instead of do time have vanished. I mean completely disappeared. Probably made chum of them on that yacht of his and scattered them at sea."

"He's not a CI?" I ask.

"No. No way. He's got some juice way up the ladder somewhere, but . . . no. He cooperates not at all."

"Does he know Brody is?"

"No."

"How do you know?"

"Because Brody is still breathing."

That's good to know—for a couple of reasons. Might be able to use it as leverage to get Brody to talk or, far more consequentially, if we find out that Brody killed Blake and can't make a case against him, Kathryn might want to let Elon know what Brody's side hustle is.

"Not much more I can tell you," he says. "But when Crews told me you were looking at him, I felt like I needed to warn you."

46

"You're not gonna believe this," Jake is saying. "I promise you that."

It's after midnight on a Thursday and Merrill and I have joined Jake in his boat along the bank between the Barge Bar and the bluff in a stand of willow trees.

My younger brother Jake and I have never been close, but for the past few years our relationship has been as good as it ever has, and I didn't hesitate to ask him to take a shift at staking out Don Richards and the Barge Bar.

He had called me as Merrill and I were sitting around a fire in my backyard and said he had something to show me. When he heard Merrill's voice he said to bring him along, that he'd like to see it too.

"Won't be the first time discernin' people don't buy the bull-shit that comes out yo mouth," Merrill says.

"What is it we're not gonna believe?" I ask.

He nods across the river to the slough where Blake's body was found.

"Little while ago," he says, "a houseboat pulled up to it. Guy dove into the river, swam to the bank, grabbed a chain hidden in some vines, pulled that tree up on a pulley, and the house-boat pulled in."

The night is dark, the stars seemingly more distant and dimmed, the muted moon a sliver behind a bank of clouds, and I have a difficult time seeing what he's describing.

"Bullshit," Merrill says.

"Knew y'all wouldn't believe me," he says. "Why y'all are here to see it for yourselves. Non-believing bastards."

Unlike previous interactions between them, their remarks are playful and lack any underlying vitriol.

We are quiet a while, waiting, our ears full of the sounds of the flowing river, the occasional splash of an unseen fish jump-ing, and the chirps and croaks and calls of the jungle-like river swamp behind us.

"Want you to know I 'ppreciate what you're doin' in the department," Jake says to Merrill.

Jake is a deputy in Dad's department where Merrill is an investigator.

"Know it ain't easy, but needs to be done. I was one of the racist, ignorant bastards, so I know."

Before Merrill can respond, the houseboat appears at the mouth of the slough and a man gets out to lift the tree just like Jake said.

"What y'all say we go have a little chat with them?" Jake says.

Without waiting for our response, he starts the motor and begins racing across the river toward the houseboat, lifting a spotlight from where it sits next to a shotgun near his feet and shining it on the houseboat as he does.

As soon as the beam from the spotlight hits the houseboat, it takes off, moving far faster than I would've said was possible.

The boat motor is loud, which with the river breeze whip-ping around our ears makes it difficult to hear.

Jake yells something to Merrill I can't make out and points to the bow of the boat.

Merrill looks around for a moment, then eventually lifts a blue emergency light, attaches it to a mount on the bow, and turns it on.

As we get closer to the houseboat, which is racing downriver now, Jake hands me the spotlight and reaches into a side compartment and pulls out a megaphone.

"Police," Jake says. "Pull over."

The motor on the houseboat is far bigger than normal, the houseboat far faster than you'd expect, but it's still a houseboat and can only go so fast.

We catch up to it and come alongside it.

Through one of the windows I see a shirtless man with long, frizzy hair wearing an old, olive-green Polish gas mask with round, oversized eyepieces and a black speech diaphragm.

"It's a meth lab," I yell.

A hatch on the roof opens and a figure wearing a Mickey Mouse mask comes up with a sawed-off shotgun and begins blasting.

Loud bangs follow rounds ricocheting around us.

The pale moonlight makes the milky Mickey look demented and deranged against the darkness of the night.

Jake lets go of the throttle, the bow of the boat dropping back into the water as the craft quickly decelerates.

As soon as the houseboat is in front of us, Jake throttles up again and cuts the boat across the wake and comes up on the other side, pulling up his shotgun as he does.

"Hey," I yell. "No need to get into a shootout with them. Let's call Fish and Game to come up on the other side and—"

Holding the shotgun with one arm, he fires a round that shatters the window on this side.

"What'd you say?" he yells. "Can't hear you over the—"

From the front of the boat Merrill begins firing rounds from his .45.

More glass shattering, wood splintering.

From somewhere in or on the houseboat I hear a wickedly gleeful maniacal cackle.

Mickey Mouse is now standing on the roof, his feet spread like a surfer attempting to maintain his balance. Apart from the large mask, the only other thing the thin, pale, hairy white man is wearing is a red mankini thong.

It's a surreal image. Mickey Mouse in a mankini with a sawed-off shotgun surfing a houseboat down the river in milky moonlight.

It's like a drug-induced Steamboat Willie nightmare straight out of the darkest regions of Walt Disney's psyche.

"The hell kinda drug fuck you up enough to wear some shit like that?" Merrill says in a moment of quiet between shots.

"They haven't invented the shit that could make me dress like that," Jake says.

As Mickey turns and levels his shotgun toward us, I pull out my 9mm and fire at him, attempting to hit his gun. He drops down, but within moments is back up again.

Merrill continues to fire through the window.

"Pull over," Jake says into the megaphone again, quickly dropping it and lifting the shotgun, pumping a shell into the chamber with one hand while operating the boat motor with the other.

As flames from a fire can be seen through the shattered windows, the houseboat suddenly lurches to the left, and Mickey Mouse loses his balance and falls into the river.

Leaving him there, Jake continues his pursuit of the houseboat, which is racing toward the left bank, the fire inside growing, intensifying, expanding.

"Slow down," I yell to Jake. "It's going to—"

The first explosion occurs then.

"*Explode*," I say.

Jake eases off the throttle. The boat slows but doesn't stop.

We are facing sideways on the river, drifting downstream and toward the left bank and the houseboat that is about to strike it.

Just before the houseboat crashes into the cypress trees lining the riverbank, two figures jump off it into the water—the long-haired Polish gas mask guy and a heavyset woman in a pink neoprene wetsuit several sizes too small for her.

As the houseboat hits the trees with a loud thwack, the two figures swim to shore, climb the hill, and disappear into the swamp.

Though the houseboat isn't moving, its motor continues to run, racing at a high-pitched whine as the propeller spins futilely in the dark water below.

In another moment, the explosions continue—three smaller ones at first, then an enormous one that engulfs the entire houseboat in flames, as Jake backs up his boat.

"Y'all want to climb the hill and chase them through the swamp?" Merrill says. "Or go pick up Mickey Mouse and make him tell us who they are and where they'll go?"

"I ain't pickin' him up," Jake says. "You saw what he was wearing."

47

"It has to be connected to Blake's death, doesn't it?" Anna is saying.

"Could be."

It's the following morning, and Anna has crawled back into bed with me after getting the kids off to school and before getting ready to go to work.

The room is cool and dim, Anna's body warm and soft beside me.

She says, "I mean, she was found behind the log they use to keep people out of their—what's back there?"

"Storage shed with meth-making supplies," I say. "They pull trailers with ATVs down a small path in the woods to it."

"Have y'all caught the other two yet?"

I shake my head. "Won't be long. A night in the river swamp and they'll be begging to be arrested."

"So they had a floating meth lab that—what?"

"Since it was mobile," I say, "they had both production and distribution in one constantly moving location, which made them harder to catch."

"Pretty ingenuous for meth heads," she says.

"*Too* ingenuous," I say.

"You think someone besides Mickey, the Pink Diver, and the Pole is behind it?"

"Almost has to be," I say.

"Were they at River Fest the year Blake was killed? Was their boat? Were they already using the slough?"

"Mickey hasn't given us much so far," I say. "He was way too high to be coherent. Hopefully, we'll get more out of him today. He's sitting in the Pine County jail. ATF is quietly working the drug side of the case, trying not to scare Richards off."

"With River Fest coming up I bet he's not going anywhere."

"What we're counting on."

"I just keep thinking Blake saw something or heard something or stumbled onto something and was killed because of it."

I nod.

"Given Brody, Kieran, and Elon's connections to drug distribution, it could've been their motive—instead of jealousy or sexual assault."

"Evidence indicates she was assaulted, and likely sexually," I say, "so it could be all of the above."

"I could see someone like Brody or Kieran but especially Elon deciding to rape her before murdering her."

I nod again. "It's . . . going to be impossible to prove . . . unless we can flip someone."

"You're gonna try to save Bri, aren't you?" she says.

I smile. "If she wasn't involved, I'd like to get her away from Elon and Brody."

"Best way to do that is by putting them in prison," she says. "But . . . you know as well as I do that she'll just go out and find another Brody and chances are he'll have an Elon in his life that he brings into hers. Unless . . ."

"Yeah?" I ask, wondering if she's thought of something potentially hopeful.

"He's both."

48

"We've got all three meth heads in custody now," Thad Jones, the Pine County sheriff's investigator is saying, "but they're refusing to talk."

I'm on the phone with Thad on my way to Kathryn's.

He didn't have to call to give me an update or keep me in the loop of what's happening with his investigation, and I'm very grateful he has.

"How bad are they hurting?" I ask.

"Bad," he says. "But not as bad as they're going to be. Give it a little while they'll be begging to talk. Give up their own mamas for a fix."

"I'd appreciate a call when they do—assuming it's Richards or DeVaughn and not their moms they give up."

"You'll be the first," he says. "Let's just get some justice for that little girl."

Jake calls and I switch over.

"Mornin' Sunshine," I say.

"Fuck you."

After just a few hours of sleep, Jake is following Dawson Lightner.

"What's he doing?" I ask.

"Probably what I want to be—sleeping. Hasn't come out of his house yet."

I wonder why he's called if Lightner has yet to even leave his house.

"But . . ." he says, "someone has gone in."

"Who?"

"Not sure. Some strung-out-looking chick. I'll try to get a pic when she comes out."

"Maybe instead of late night, he does early morning booty calls."

"Great way to start the day," he says, "but I'll be shocked if that's what she's here for. If she is we're gonna need better words than *reacher* and *settler*."

"What does she look like?"

"Mid-thirties, maybe—though she looks like she's pushing sixty," he says. "Blond hair and big tits. Lots of makeup and jewelry.

"Sounds like Tasha Woods," I say.

"One of your old girlfriends?"

"Bartender at the Barge Bar."

"So a coworker of Dawson's."

"Yeah," I say. "They're probably just having a staff meeting. Let me know what happens."

49

"What if we can't get them for murder, but get them nonetheless?" I ask Kathryn.

"What do you mean?"

"Could you be satisfied if we send them to prison on drug charges?"

"I want to know who did it and why," she says. "That's more important to me than their punishment. But I've about given up on ever even knowing that."

"I haven't," I say. "Not yet. But . . . so many mistakes were made in the original investigation—"

"Like what—not investigating?" she says.

"Makes everything more difficult than it has to be and making a case nearly impossible."

"Are you quitting?"

"Absolutely not," I say.

"Then—"

"Came to give you an update and let you know about what went down last night—"

"What happened last night?"

"But as I was driving over I had the thought that our best

hope of justice at this point is seeing these guys go down for some of their other crimes."

"Have you given up on figuring out what happened and who's responsible?"

"I haven't given up on anything," I say. "I'm just asking what possible outcomes you would find satisfying. It'd be one thing if the initial investigation misinterpreted evidence, but they didn't even collect it, didn't treat anything like it was evidence, so we have nothing to build a case on."

"I've told you. I don't care about being able to make a case in court. Well, I care about it, but not as much as knowing what happened and looking her killer in the eye and asking him why. But it sounds like you've given up on giving me even that."

"I haven't given up and I won't. I told you that."

"Yeah, but now you're sounding more like those police departments, the way a case is still open and active but it's obvious they have no actual hope of ever closing it."

"That's not what it's like at all," I say. "But . . . my leave time is coming to an end, and when I return to work I'll have less time to devote to it and—"

"Would you be saying any of this if you knew for sure she was your daughter?"

"You're not listening to what I'm saying."

"It's not so much what you're saying as how you're saying it. You sound discouraged and defeated and—"

"I'm just tired. Don't let my fatigue make you think I'm giving up. I'm not. I'm just updating you on everything and trying to give you an accurate view of where we are right now."

"So what happened last night? Why are you so tired?"

I tell her.

"You think they had something to do with it?"

"It's possible," I say. "Not sure yet. But the fact that her body was found in their—"

"Are they connected to Brody or Bri or Kieran? Could they all be in it together?"

"We just don't know yet. They could be. It's also possible they knew about the meth lab's connection to that slough and that's why they placed her body over there."

"See? You're making progress."

"I never said I wasn't. The progress is part of the reason I'm tired."

"You're not quitting, are you?"

"That's what I've been saying. And there's more."

"*More?*"

"I spoke to Bri, Brody, and Elon DeVaughn yesterday."

"*What?* Talk about burying the lead. How? Where? What'd they say?"

I tell her.

"Oh, my God. That's so . . . I can't believe she talked to you."

"I think I know a way to get all of them to talk more—or at least Bri and Brody. I wanted to see how you'd feel about it."

"Tell me."

"I want to get everyone together," I say. "See what happens."

"How? Where?"

"The barge and the cliffside."

"They'll never go for that."

"They might," I say. "If you tell them that in exchange for their participation and cooperation you'll drop the wrongful death suit."

50

"You just don't quit, do you?"

I am standing at the open door of Brody and Bri's condo, Brody shaking his head at me from the other side.

I have come in person instead of calling because I want to see Bri to make sure she's okay.

"I have something to say you're going to want to hear. Can I come in?"

He frowns.

"It's good news about the wrongful death suit," I say. "It'll only take a minute."

"If you're lyin', I swear to God ..."

He steps aside and lets me in.

I walk down the short entryway into the small, open living, dining, and kitchen area, my shoes clicking on the white tile floor.

Bri, who is lying on the couch, stands. "John? What're you doing here?"

I look at her closely, examine her for any signs of injury, watching her movements for any indication of pain.

"She's fine," Brody says. "I haven't laid a finger on her and I never will. The only girl I ever put my hands on like that was that crazy bitch Claire, and she did more damage to me than I did to her. I would never hurt Bri and I won't let anyone else do it either—not even Elon." He looks over at her. "Tell him."

"He's good to me," she says. "He's never hurt me."

"Where is Elon?" I ask.

"Don't know," Brody says. "Went out. What did you want to tell us?"

"Would you like some tea or something?" Bri asks.

"Thank you," I say. "I'm fine."

"Do you want to sit down?" she says.

"This'll only take a minute."

"Then get to it," Brody says.

"Blake's mom just wants this to be over," I say.

"We do too," Bri says.

"If you guys would be willing to come to a gathering of some of the people who were at River Fest the year Blake was killed—"

"She wasn't killed," Brody says. "She died."

"If y'all would be willing to come and cooperate—answer questions, give information, tell the truth—she'll drop the wrongful death suit."

"Oh, that's great," Bri says. "That's . . . I've been wanting to talk to her anyway. I feel so . . . bad. Would love to get to tell her how sorry I am and—"

"No way," Brody says. "No fuckin' way."

"I get you not being willing to do it if you have something to hide," I say.

"Haven't had shit to hide for five years and I've been hounded like a fuckin' serial killer."

"This is your chance to end all that," I say. "If you weren't involved in Blake's murder or covering it up in some way, you have nothing to fear. All I'm after is the truth. Have no desire to falsely accuse anybody or—"

He shakes his head. "There's no upside. No—"

"I have no jurisdiction there," I say, "no official role in this case. It's just a discussion about what happened to Blake and a memorial where she died that she never got to have."

Bri says, "Yeah, that would be nice. She needs that. We need that. You tell Miss Kathryn I'll be there."

It's a good sign that Bri is willing to go without Brody, without his blessing or permission. She must not be as controlled by him as I had believed.

"It's some kind of trick, Bri," Brody says.

"I don't think it is, Brody."

"I give you my word it's not," I say.

"*Your word*?" Brody says.

"My word," I say. "It's all the assurance you need. And if you were a different sort of man, you'd know that."

"I believe him," Bri says. "I trust him. I'm going."

51

A s I'm walking to my truck, I check my phone and see I have two messages from Jake.

"Dawson's going on the river," he says. "It's gonna be harder to follow him without being seen, but I'm gonna try. Call me back."

I press the button to call Jake back. It rings several times then goes to voicemail.

I play the next message.

"Dawson went to the barge. He's on it now. Haven't seen anyone else yet, but . . . there's a . . . Never seen such a big-ass boat on the river. It's like a . . . I guess it's a yacht. Kind of thing you'd see in the gulf or bay, not the river. I'm gonna see if I can sneak aboard the barge and try to see what they're up to. Call me back."

I call him back again as I jump into my truck and race toward the river.

After several rings, the call goes to voicemail again.

I click off and call Merrill.

"Jake followed Lightner to the barge and now he's not

answering," I say. "I think Elon is there too. Can you meet me at the landing with a boat?"

"On my way."

I continue to try Jake as I speed toward the landing, but he never answers.

When I reach the landing, Merrill already has the boat in the water waiting on me.

Jumping out of my truck, I run down the gangway, across the floating wooden dock, and bound into the boat. He guns the throttle of the idling motor and we rush downriver as fast as the small fishing craft will take us.

As we near the Barge Bar, I see Jake's boat moored to one of the slips, but there is no sign of DeVaughn's yacht.

Merrill maneuvers the boat into the slip closest to the ladder on this side, we quickly tie it to the dock, and sprint down the catwalk and up the ladder.

Withdrawing our weapons, we scan the deck and then enter the cargo containers that make up the inside part of the bar.

Inside the bar, we find Dawson unconscious on the floor, traces of blood in his hair where he was struck on the head.

As Merrill continues to search for Jake, I attempt to revive Dawson.

He moans and opens his eyes for a moment, then closes them again.

"Dawson, wake up. Where is Jake? What happened?"

"Huh? John? What is— Hey, Elon DeVaughn has your brother."

He tries to sit up, but his eyes roll back in his head, and he falls back to the floor.

"Be careful. He's armed. He's on his yacht . . . Bet he's headed toward the bay."

Merrill reappears.

"Far as I can tell, nobody else on the barge," he says. "Quarters and cargo bay below are empty. But they's another boat besides his and Jake's tied up to the other side."

"Don Richards," Dawson says. "If he's not here, DeVaughn must have him too."

Before Dawson has finished speaking, Merrill is on his radio requesting backup—both here and downriver toward the bay.

"DeVaughn is dangerous," Dawson says.

"Notice he left your ass alive," Merrill says.

"I don't think he . . . He wasn't the one who hit me. I think it was Don. But . . . I'm not sure."

I know we should do a more thorough search of the barge, but with backup on the way and with even the possibility of DeVaughn having Jake, all I can think about is getting back to the boat and pursuing the yacht.

"Backup will be here in a few minutes," I say to Dawson. "Stay here and wait for them. Tell them everything."

"I'm going with—"

He tries to sit up but falls back again.

Without another word, Merrill and I are running out of the bar.

When we reach the deck, Merrill says, "Go left."

Without hesitation I do.

We run across the deck, toward the ladder on the left side.

"Don's got himself a go-fast boat. Be our only chance of catching the yacht."

52

I f there was ever any question about Don Richards being a drug dealer before, his Nor-Tech 450 Sport CC leaves no doubt.

The forty-five-foot-long center-console go-fast boat with its five Mercury Racing Verado 400R outboards on the back is exactly the type of craft a modern-day rumrunner would have.

Capable of speeds of over eighty miles per hour, this overkill craft should have no problem catching DeVaughn's yacht.

Merrill drives it like a kid on Christmas morning—not smoothly, not expertly, but enthusiastically, recklessly.

I've never been on a boat even half this fast, and I hang on with both hands as I scan the wide river in front of us, searching for signs of DeVaughn.

I have no idea how much of a head start the yacht has, but whatever it is, it won't be enough.

The afternoon sky is clear, the sun bright, visibility excellent.

The serpentine river is wide and open, the sunlight

refracting off its smooth greenish-brown surface in shimmering, dancing waves.

As if a hovercraft, the speedboat is flying so fast it seems not to be touching the water.

Merrill yells, "Za ask you for gift ideas for Christmas or my birthday . . ." nodding toward the boat beneath him with a huge smile on his face.

"Pretty sure this one will be available at police auction pretty soon," I shout. "If it survives this particular pursuit."

"Oh, it'll—"

As we round the bend, DeVaughn's yacht comes into view.

I can't tell how fast it's going, but compared to us, it appears to be standing still.

Merrill finds another gear and within another couple of minutes we're coming up alongside the yacht.

DeVaughn is standing behind the windshield, his hands on the steering wheel.

There is no sign of Jake.

Merrill slows to match DeVaughn's pace.

As I pull my weapon out and point it at DeVaughn, I notice Merrill has done the same, steering the boat with one hand now.

DeVaughn jerks the wheel hard to the right, slamming the bow of his boat into ours.

Merrill and I grab onto the nearest solid object and steady ourselves as he rights the boat.

DeVaughn disappears into the cabin below.

"Can you bring us alongside it close enough for me to jump?"

"The hell kinda question is that?" he says. "'Course I can."

He steers the boat over next to the yacht, bumping it a time or two and drifting away before steadying it at a distance I can make the jump.

Holding on to the windshield, I climb up and step out onto the gunwale.

Pumping my arms for propulsion, I bend my knees into a deep squat and spring up, leaping as long as I can.

I land on the small dive platform off the stern.

The plastic platform is wet and my feet slip.

My feet come out from underneath me and I land hard on my back.

The vibrations of the engine rattle through me and I can hear the propeller beneath the platform, see the churning of the river water just below my feet.

I can feel myself sliding off and flail about, searching for something to hold on to.

Just as I'm about to go into the water, and possibly into the propeller, my right hand finds a mooring cleat and I grab it hard, gripping it with all the strength in my hand and pulling myself back onto the boat.

As I crawl from the dive platform into the boat, I pull my gun.

When I push myself up to my feet, DeVaughn is standing there with Jake.

Jake's head and face are bloodied and bruised, his hair wet with sweat. His hands are cuffed in front of him. The civilian clothes he's wearing are torn and ripped and smeared with blood.

DeVaughn has a huge serrated-edge hunting knife pressed against the side of Jake's neck with his right hand, his left arm around Jake's chest, a 9mm in his left hand.

"I can kill both of y'all at the same time," DeVaughn says. "Drop your gun."

I shake my head. "So you can kill both of us at the same time? I don't think so. You're the one with the choice to make. You can die here today or you can go to prison and eventually get out and hurt some more people. Up to you."

Merrill bumps the boat and we all have to shift our feet and move our arms to keep from falling.

As he does, I catch Jake's eye and give him the subtlest of signs with my eyes.

"He does that again and I'm gonna cut your brother's head off. Now, lower your goddamn gun."

"Okay. Okay," I say, bending over and holding my gun out. "Merrill, don't hit the boat again. I'm putting my gun down and . . ."

Merrill rams the boat again—much harder this time—and we all lose our balance. But DeVaughn far more than me and Jake since we were expecting it.

Jake drops his head down and rears it back as hard as he can, striking DeVaughn in the face before dropping to the deck.

Blood spurts out from DeVaughn's broken nose and he grabs at it as Merrill and I both fire.

Neither round finds its target.

DeVaughn drops to the deck and I dive on top of him, striking his hands with the butt of my gun, knocking his weapons away.

Punching him in the nose to further subdue him, I holster my weapon and withdraw my handcuffs from my belt.

Flipping him over, I pry his hands away from his nose and cuff them behind him.

"How the hell'd you both miss?" Jake says.

"I's aiming for you," Merrill says.

53

"So was Dawson at the wrong place at the wrong time or is he involved?" Anna asks.

And with that single question everything falls into place.

I stop. *The wrong place at the wrong time.*

Anna and I are out for a walk. It's evening and the sidewalks along Main Street are peaceful, the gold magic-hour glow of sunset suffusing everything with a quiet calm.

The kids, including Johanna who is with us for the weekend, are at home, practicing being rock stars.

"What is it?" she asks.

"Sorry," I say. "I was just—your question made me think about the case. I need to look back at a few things, but you may've just given me the missing piece. Thank you."

"Happy to help. Do you want to go look up what you need to?"

I shake my head. "Nah, it can wait. I'll do it after you go to sleep."

"You get up to all sorts of things while I'm sleeping, don't you?"

"I am the night," I say. "Back to your question—I'm leaning toward Dawson being involved, but I've got to look up a few things to be sure."

"Jake is always in the wrong place at the wrong time," she says.

I laugh. "Came pretty close to being the last time."

"For you too," she says, squeezing my hand. "I can't even imagine life without you. Please be more careful. Take fewer risks."

"I am. I will. Coming home to you and the kids is far, far more important to me than catching the worst bad guy ever."

"Speaking of bad guys," she says. "What about Richards? Where was he?"

"His body was found floating near the north side of the barge. Stabbed to death. Early theory is DeVaughn killed him and stole all his product. DeVaughn's yacht was filled with it. But I'm not so sure. It'll be Merrill's case. He'll figure it out."

"And if he can't," she says, "he can always get some help from Jasper Wallace."

I laugh out loud at that.

54

On the weekend when River Fest should be happening, we gather beneath a blood-red sky on the deck of the Barge Bar to, I hope, bring closure to the case.

"This sky reminds me of the one the evening Blake's body was discovered," Addie remarks to no one in particular.

Since Anna's comment about *wrong place wrong time,* I had been thinking about and looking at the evidence within a new paradigm, and I believe I know what happened to Blake and who's responsible.

We've invited everyone we could find who was here the night Blake was killed—and most of them showed up.

Anna and Merrill are at a table close to where I'm standing in front of the gathered group.

Cameron and Hailey Perry are at a table next to them, holding hands and looking happier than either of them was the last time I saw them.

Kathryn is at a table next to them with Addie, Alex, Claire, and Corbin, who after running around the deck is now asleep in her arms.

Behind them at a table by himself, with a bandage on his head, is Dawson Lightner.

Next to him, Bri, Brody, and Kieran at a table of their own. Kieran is here through a furlough arranged with PCI.

Across from them with two empty tables in between, a cuffed and shackled Elon DeVaughn sits with the deputy whose custody he's in.

Will Crews from Bridgeport PD and Thad Jones from the Pine County Sheriff's Department are at a table on the other side of them.

Tasha Woods, the Barge Bar bartender, sits at a table by herself in the back.

Not far from her, Frida Price, the PI from Panama City, sits with someone I don't recognize, as if she thought her invitation included a plus one.

In the center of them all sitting in chairs not near a table, Trevor King sits with Missy Arnold, his ex-girlfriend at the time of Blake's death who he is now back together with.

Standing over to the side, as if observing and not participating, Dad, Jake, and Jasper are in street clothes.

"I've asked you all here this evening—"

Bri stands up and raises her hand.

"Before you start, can I say something?"

"Sure."

"I just want you to know, Miss Kathryn, how sorry I am for everything."

Kathryn turns toward her.

"I don't know how we got to where we are, but . . ." She starts crying. "I'm . . . I'm sorry for my part. And I'm sorry for not coming to the funeral. I was . . . I was trying to be respectful. I knew you blamed me and I figured you didn't want me there. That's what other people told me. Anyway, I'm sorry. I love you and I loved Blake and I miss her every day and I wish I had never taken her with me."

She sits back down. Brody remains rigid beside her.

The evening is unseasonably cool, the soft sun blanketing the river and the swamps with an orange-gold glow and burnishing the tops of the trees along the western horizon.

"I've asked you all to join me here this evening not to make an arrest—there's not enough evidence for that and I have no jurisdiction here—but to honor Blake and give witness to what happened to her and why. I'm going to share with you who I believe killed her and why they did it, in hopes of removing the insidious torture of not knowing and perhaps some of the grief from this giving mother."

I pause as people shift in their seats and an awkwardness descends on the crowd.

"But before I do that," I say, "I want to give the killer a chance to confess. To stand up right now and confess to this community what you did and why you did it. It's the single most important thing you could do for the sake of your own soul as well as the heart of Blake's mom."

I wait.

As I scan the crowd, very few make eye contact with me, and most people are looking around at each other.

"Please," I say. "Take responsibility for what you did. Show compassion for your victim's mother and loved ones."

No one moves.

"Okay," I say. "But I think you're making a huge mistake."

I wait one moment longer.

"The first question to answer is whether Blake's death was accidental," I say. "And in a way it was."

"See?" Jasper says. "I told y'all—"

"He already said her killer is here," Jake says.

"She was killed," Dawson says. "It wasn't an accident. I'll go to my grave believing that."

"And I'll go to my grave knowing it was an accident," Jasper says. "So where does that leave us?"

"I'm convinced that Blake did not die as the result of an accidental fall from the side of that cliff," I say, nodding over toward it. "If you fall from up there, you land on the ledge—and even if you try to say that she could've fallen onto the ledge, hit her head, and then stood up dazed and somehow fell the rest of the way, it wouldn't account for her injuries. If she fell from either side of the cliff—while going to pee or something—the trees and underbrush would've stopped her within a few feet. No way she makes it to the water. No way she sustains the injuries that she had. Frida Price and Dawson Lightner proved that."

They both nod their appreciation for the recognition.

"And if it wasn't an accident, then the question becomes who killed her," I say. "And with all the drug-related activity going on with Don Richards and Elon DeVaughn and others, did that have anything to do with why she died? Or was it a boyfriend who claimed he didn't get her text asking him to come get her when we know he did?"

"I didn't," Trevor says. "I swear it. My phone was in the living room. Someone had opened the text before I woke up the next morning and saw it, but it wasn't me. I swear to God."

I look at Missy. Trevor follows my gaze.

"Don't look at me," she says. "I don't look at other people's phones."

"Did an older authority figure who seemed too attentive go too far with his attention and—"

"That's sick," Dawson says, "and I can't believe you'd even suggest something like that, John. I thought you—"

"Did the guys she was camping with up on that cliff, drugged-up and overwrought, sexually assault her and kill her to cover it up? Or did the other girl up there go crazy with jealousy and alcohol-rage and attempt to eliminate the competition?"

"I would never do anything like that," Bri says.

"What?" Claire says. "Assault someone out of jealous rage?"

"That's different."

"Or did her ex have something to do with it—whether she went willingly to meet him or not? Or perhaps did his girlfriend at the time, now his wife, catch them together and exact her revenge? There seems to be no end of suspects and motives."

"She fell off that cliff," Jasper says again. "It's—"

"Not only did she not fall off the bluff into the river, but her body didn't float over into the slough. It's impossible given the current."

"There's always things you can't explain in a homicide," Jasper says. "Everybody knows that."

"Sure," I say, "but let's talk about what we can explain. The autopsy indicates Blake was assaulted."

"No," Jasper says, "the ME said she was—"

"I'm not talking about the erroneous conclusions he reached in his report that was meant to back your conclusion of accidental death. I'm talking about the evidence of the autopsy itself. We can also explain with reasonable certainty the triangular impression left in her chest," I say. "It was made by the canoe used to move her body over to the slough."

"*Our* canoe?" Bri says, then looks from Brody to Kieran to Elon nearby.

"Yes," I say.

"No," she says. "No way. We didn't—"

"Told you it was a setup," Brody says.

"John," Bri says, hurt in her voice, "I thought you were different. We didn't have anything to do with her death."

"Actually, you did," I say, "but I don't think you even know it."

"I didn't," she says. "I swear it. I . . . How? How did I?"

"By letting her borrow your clothes and changing your sleeping arrangements on Saturday night," I say.

"I don't understand," she says.

"Don't you?" I say. "You were the intended victim. Not Blake. The killer came to kill you, not—"

"Who?" she says. "Who tried to kill me? Who killed Blake?"

"Claire," I say. "The young woman Brody strung along and who thought she was going to be with him at River Fest. The young woman pregnant with his child."

"That's my son?" Brody says, looking over at Corbin.

Everyone else, including Kathryn, is looking at Claire.

Claire doesn't say anything, just begins crying quietly.

"The young woman you humiliated and assaulted," I continue. "The young woman who left—went home Friday night, but came back on Saturday, plotting her revenge. The young woman who had been you the year before, who had been up on the cliff and knew how to get back. The young woman who had such a turbulent, obsessive, and violent relationship with Brody that only the shock and horror of accidentally killing her friend could make her walk away for good. The young woman who pretended to make up with you—and even bought y'all a make-up drink that she spiked so y'all'd be sleeping heavily when she came to call. The young woman who overheard y'all discussing the sleeping arrangements and thought you'd be outside and Blake in the tent. Kieran's spiked drink had the most in it and made it so he couldn't even climb back up the cliff when y'all arrived. But . . . Blake's . . . Blake's was spilled when Dawson bumped into her, which is what made her wear your clothes and which is why at some point after Claire had bashed her head in with a blunt object of some kind, she woke up enough to fight back. But it was too late to turn back then, wasn't it?"

I look at her.

Her eyes widen and fill with panic, her gaze shifting around to the others. She looks like she wants to run, but is trapped by the child in her lap and being on a barge in the middle of the river.

"She had brain damage," she finally says. "Her head was . . . I . . . It happened so fast . . . I just saw the clothes, thought it was Bri. I bashed her head in with a . . . huge, heavy rock."

Continuing to hold her sleeping child in her arms, she remains still and speaks softly.

"Claire, no," Kathryn says. "Please, God, no."

"She was . . . already gone," she continues, breaking down as she does. "Oh God, it was so . . . horrible. I never meant to . . . I loved her. She was my friend. I . . . Miss Kathryn, I'm so, so sorry. I . . . I went up there to get back at . . . at her. I was so . . . humiliated and . . . I couldn't see straight. I wasn't going to let that piece of shit treat me like that, to . . . I was carrying his . . . his baby. And she was going to treat me like that . . . And he was going to discard me like that. No. I wasn't having it. I was going to . . . I wanted them both to pay . . . and for him to be with me and our . . . son. I . . . I didn't see Kieran in the canoe. If I had . . . I might have known that Blake was not in the tent, but . . . I saw Bri's clothes and . . . I was already . . . I had taken some speed earlier and then paddling over and climbing the bluff . . . I was so wired. I just went crazy. But . . . I was getting back at Bri. Bri not Blake."

"You weren't getting back at her," Kathryn says. "You were killing her. At some point you knew it was Blake and . . . and you didn't stop."

"I couldn't. It was too late. I'm not a bad person. I'm not. I just . . . I had to—"

"No," Kathryn says. "No. You didn't have to. You didn't have to do any of this. And once you saw it was her, you could've stopped. You could've . . . let me . . . have my daughter back . . . Even if she was damaged. But you kept going. And you covered it all up."

"After you finished her off," I say, "you gave her injuries to make it look like she had been raped."

Kathryn says, "How did you even know how to—"

"Yeah, Brody," Claire says, "how did I know what those marks look like?"

"You murdered my Blake," Kathryn says. "You—"

"I didn't mean to."

"No," Bri says, "you crazy bitch, you meant to murder me."

"It wasn't me," she says. "That's not who I am. I just went . . . I don't know. It was like I was possessed. It was because of all the shit he put me through."

"But you were killing me to get him back."

She opens her mouth but nothing comes out.

Eventually, she says, "I snapped. I panicked. Some other part of me took over. It wasn't me. It . . . I don't know. I can't explain it."

"After she was dead," I say, "did you drag and roll her body down the hill or did you throw her off the side?"

"It wasn't her," she says. "It was just her body. She was gone. I . . . I threw her off. But . . . She landed on the ledge. I had to climb down there and drag her over to the side of the hill and pull and roll her down from there."

"And at some point Kieran woke up and started up the hill," I say.

She nods. "I was coming down the hill with her as he was coming up. I rolled her over and we hid several feet off the trail to let him pass."

Her use of *we hid* makes it sound like something they were doing together.

"Then you went down and got Blake's body into the canoe and paddled her over to the slough on the other side of the river," I say.

"I . . . I knew the longer it was . . . before she was . . . found . .

. the harder it would be to tell what happened. And the farther away I could be."

"You did all that to my baby," Kathryn says. "To your friend."

"I'm so, so sorry, but—"

"But what? How can you possibly justify what you did?"

"I loved her," she says. "And she loved me. She wouldn't want us both to lose our lives if we didn't have to. She wouldn't. She would want me to be able to raise my child."

Kathryn starts crying.

Addie says, "You didn't deserve her as a friend."

"I know. I know that better than you can imagine."

"All this time," Kathryn says. "All this time you've been by my side, so supportive, so helpful in trying to find out what happened to Blake . . . and all this time you've known. You've seen my agony. You've seen how much I needed to know what really happened to her."

I say, "All this time . . . she's been pointing a finger at Brody."

"Yeah," Addie says. "What? Were you going to let him go to prison for it if . . ."

Claire doesn't say anything.

"Were you hoping I'd leave him if he went to prison?" Bri says. "So you could get back with him?"

Claire shrugs. "I . . . I don't know. I didn't think it—I didn't plan that far."

Kathryn turns to Bri. "I'm sorry for believing you had something to do with it. I—"

"It's okay. I'm sorry I didn't handle it better. I should've . . . There's so much I should've done."

"Every one of you bastards thought I had killed her," Brody says. "Y'all owe us an—"

"Before you get too righteous and outraged," I say, "I don't think any of this would've happened if you hadn't treated Claire the way you did. If Bri hadn't assaulted her. And if you hadn't been camping up there on that cliff."

"You sayin'—"

"He sayin'," Merrill says, "maybe save the demands for apologies."

"Whatever you say I done, it wasn't as bad as what y'all thought I done."

"Okay," Addie says. "We'll give you that. But let that be enough. This ain't about you."

He starts to respond, but stops and nods.

Kathryn begins to cry even harder, a deep soul-sob that seems to involve some release and relief at finally knowing the truth.

As she does, Addie and Alex and Bri and Trevor and Cameron and Hailey and Dawson gather around her, hugging and comforting her and each other, and shedding tears of their own.

55

"I was wrong," Dad says, "and I'm sorry."

I nod, but don't say anything, still feeling guarded around him.

Most of the group is gone. The few that remain mill about, talking and hugging each other. Jasper talks to Jake while Dad talks to me. None of us hug each other.

"I had some reasons for what I did that I haven't shared with anyone," he says, glancing back over his shoulder at Jasper and Jake, "but . . . if I had thought for a minute that it was murder, I never would've . . . I honestly thought it was an accident. I never saw the autopsy photos back then. If I had . . ."

He looks tired and even older tonight, and maybe even a little weak and infirmed, and I wonder if his health issues have resurfaced.

"I never thought you were knowingly covering up a murder," I say.

"But you did think I was covering up shoddy police work, didn't you?"

I shrug. "Why did you cover for Jasper?"

"He was young and had a drinking problem," he says. "Reminded me of you."

My eyes sting and I blink several times.

"I was trying to help him, but . . . He's not you . . . nothing like you . . . and . . . The thing is . . . once I found out that Brody was a CI and I knew those other agencies were involved . . . I thought if there was a real problem with the investigation, they'd find it. And the truth is . . . I was . . . lost . . . just sort of floundering. I hadn't lost an election in decades. I was hurt and mad and . . . I passed the buck. I just told you I didn't even look at the autopsy photos. There's no excuse. I'm ashamed of myself. And I just want you to know it."

I'm not sure what to say.

I nod and swallow. "I understand," is all I manage.

"I appreciate what you did here today," he says. "You cleaned up a mess I made and I want you to know I appreciate it and tell you I'm sorry for how I acted."

Jasper walks up. "Well, I ain't sorry," he says. "Didn't do anything wrong. I went with what it looked like and what I had to go on. And even if I had done a deeper investigation, I wouldn't've come up with any of this shit you said this evening. No one would have."

"Someone did," Dad says.

56

"What you've done for me . . ." Kathryn says, shaking her head. "I . . . can't even begin to thank you for . . ."

It's a while later—after many tears and much consoling and comforting.

Most everyone has gone, but there are still a few people milling about.

Kathryn and I are standing apart from the others over near the storage containers that make up the indoor part of the bar.

Her eyes are clear as though the multitude of tears has cleansed both them and the soul beyond them, and her countenance has been lifted in a way I hadn't thought possible.

She knows the truth and it has set her free in a way, and she has been comforted by the community formed and connected by the loss of her daughter.

"What you've done for our . . . for Blake."

"I'm happy to have . . . helped," I say, "but so many were involved."

"I know, and please let them know how grateful I am, how . . . much their . . . contributions mean to me."

"I will."

"Anna, Merrill, and Jake in particular," she says.

I nod.

"Next to . . . bringing her back . . . this is the best thing y'all could've done for me. And to . . . put someone like Elon DeVaughn away too is just . . . And I think you have saved Cam and Hailey's marriage also."

If it is saved it will be because they saved it, but I know what she means and just nod. Though it has the most direct impact on Kathryn, knowing what happened, who was responsible, and why it was done seems to have removed the dark cloud hanging over everyone connected to the case.

"What's going to happen to . . ."

I know who she's talking about. I also know she doesn't want to say her name.

Claire had been among the first to leave, carrying her still sleeping son as she did.

"I'm not sure anything will," I say. "We can push for the DA to bring a case against her and hope she's willing to formally confess on record, accept a plea deal, but . . . I can't see her cooperating, not when it could mean losing her son."

"I don't even care," she says. "This was never about vengeance. The not knowing was driving me crazy. I say I don't care. I . . . actually . . . part of me wants her to suffer horribly and die, but it's a relatively small part."

"You can push for them to move forward with charges," I say. "And even if she's never convicted . . . there's a certain public accountability that comes with just being charged."

"I'll think about it."

We are silent a moment, the river flowing gently around us, the swamps lining it calm and quiet in the gloaming.

"I've been thinking . . ." she says. "I haven't really touched anything in Blake's room. Her DNA has to be all over it. Her hairbrush alone must have . . . If you'd like to do a test to see if you were her . . ."

I shake my head. "I'm already grieving for her like she is."

I've thought about it a lot, and as much as part of me wants to know, needs to know, another part of me knows that knowing wouldn't change anything, wouldn't serve any purpose unrelated to ego.

I spend my life attempting to answer questions and solve mysteries, afflicted with the insatiable thirst of needing to know. But I have learned how little there is we can ever really truly know. Life's greatest mysteries can't be solved. Life itself is a mystery—not a vague unknown but a specific unknowable. In my capacity as a spiritual seeker and a detective, I bear witness to the Mystery. I am humbled and instructed by it, and I've come to realize that questions themselves are answers, and embracing ambiguity is the deeper, more peaceful path.

The intellectual puzzles certain crimes provide pale in comparison to the mysteries of existence, of life and death, and of the nature of the human and the divine.

I have investigated as if I'm Blake's father, and I'm grieving as if I am. How would the confirmation of a paternity test alter that in any way? For the rest of my life, I'm going to live with what might have been—and do my best to allow that reality to do its deep soul work in me instead of becoming a tormenting intellectual obsession.

She nods. "Okay. I . . . I certainly understand. If you ever change your mind and want to know . . . As you've proven to me today . . . knowing is better. Speaking of . . . I know I will always wonder what might have been when it comes to us—what you and I might've had, what Blake's life would've been like if you had been in it, but . . . know this . . . I'll keep that to myself and I'll . . . I'm going to leave you alone. You've done so much for me —not just this time . . . but before. And not just me but my family. Thank you and take good care of yourself—not just everybody else."

"**I**s it okay to say I hope she means it?" Anna says. "That she'll really leave you alone."

"Of course," I say. "You can say and hope anything you want. Especially as it relates to me."

We are driving back on a peaceful evening, the last of the setting sun backlighting the pines before us, on our way to pick up the kids from Dad and Verna's.

"I'm happy your interaction with her is over," she says, "and that you're going home with me."

"Me too," I say. "I'm always happy when I go home with or to you. You and our kids *are* my home."

"I could tell you this every day," she says, "and I should. I should tell you far more than I do, but . . . you are . . . absolutely amazing and I am so proud of you."

"Thank you," I say. "That's—"

"The gift you just gave not only Kathryn but everyone involved . . . and you've done that for so very many grieving family members and loved ones over the years."

I take in a breath and take in what she's saying and feel full —seen, appreciated, loved.

With homicides, you can never do what the family most wants—bring their loved one back—so the best to ever hope for is the chance to provide some comfort, a few answers, and occasionally a measure of some kind of justice.

"And you were hot doing it," she says, "which is just a plus —a plus for me, not Kathryn or anyone else."

"I'm glad you think so," I say. "And everything I am is for you, not anyone else."

"I was thinking . . ." she says. "Well, initially I was thinking we could go home first and pick up the kids from Verna a little later, but I can't wait that long . . . So . . . why don't you find us a dirt road to pull down and let me show you just how much you turn me on?"

I do.

And she does.

And it's the single best remuneration of any investigation I've ever received.

JOIN MY VIP READERS' GROUP

Join my VIP Readers' Group Today by going to http://www.
michaellister.com/contact and receive free books, news and
updates, and great mystery and crime recommendations.